The Bounty Trail

The Bounty Trail

L.D. TETLOW

A Black Horse Western

ROBERT HALE · LONDON

ISBN 0 7090 6767 4

Robert Hale Limited
Clerkenwell House
Clerkenwell Green
London EC1R 0HT

BBRA		BCRO	
BASH		BGRE	
BBIN		BHAR	
BBIR		BSAN	
BCON		BWHI	ozlo

Typeset by
Derek Doyle & Associates, Liverpool.
Printed and bound in Great Britain by
Antony Rowe Limited, Wiltshire

ONE

Caleb Black, part-time preacher and full time bounty hunter, black by name and black by colour, studied the various Wanted posters pinned to the board outside the sheriff's office. There were five of them, three of which were for small-time local criminals for whom the total reward was only $200. In other circumstances Caleb would have been satisfied with this meagre amount but on this occasion his interest was very definitely in the other two posters.

'Nathaniel Parker, one thousand dollars,' Caleb muttered to himself. 'Commonly known as Clubfoot Parker. Vincent Smith, better known as Vinny Smith, also one thousand. I reckon I know just where to find them.'

His mind went back two days to when he had called in at a trading post-cum-saloon on the edge of a forest. Two men matching the descriptions of Parker and Smith had been propping up the bar and appeared to be in deep conversation with the owner of the trading post – one Ephram Barnes. Ephram Barnes was plainly the result of a liaison between white and black parents, a fact he seemed to resent.

He had greeted Caleb with hostility, stating that blacks were not welcome in his establishment. When Caleb had pointed out Ephram's obvious background, he had reacted by venting his anger against his mother.

'Stupid cow got herself took by some passin' runaway slave,' he had rasped. 'I can't help what happened.'

'Just as I can't help being the colour I am,' retorted Caleb. 'The difference seems to be that I'm proud of my birthright. However, I will not force myself upon someone who does not want me. I shall be on my way just as soon as I have had something to eat. I've been travelling for six days and this is the first chance I have had of a decent meal. I take it you do provide food?'

'I got stew an' dumplin's,' replied Ephram. 'Don't ask me what's in the stew, that's my woman's department.'

'Stew and dumplings sounds just fine to me,' said Caleb. He turned to look at the other two men as Ephram went to inform his woman that she had a customer. 'Good afternoon, gentlemen,' nodded Caleb. 'Perhaps you could tell me where the nearest town is?'

'Pretty fancy talkin' for a negro,' replied one of the men. 'Pretty fancy clothes too. Last time I saw duds like them it was on a preacher. Where'd you steal 'em from?'

'I am not in the habit of stealing anything,' said Caleb. 'I wear these clothes because I am a preacher.'

'I don't reckon there's much call for black preachers in these parts,' said the second man.

'Ephram's the only coloured feller for miles around an' he's only tolerated 'cos he lives out here. You say you're a preacher, since when did preachers carry guns, especially nice lookin' pieces like the one you got?'

'In a perfect world there would be no need for anyone to carry guns,' said Caleb. 'Unfortunately the world is far from perfect and I find a gun necessary for my own protection.'

He had made no effort to hide the fact that there was a pistol attached to his right thigh, he never did. However, he was always very careful not to expose an identical pistol on his left thigh. He always ensured that his long coat covered this side. Any man, especially a black preacher, wearing two guns was a rarity and that fact had saved his life on more than one occasion. His adversaries had always made the mistake of assuming that, once they had forced him to discard the one gun, he was unarmed.

Both men studied Caleb for a few moments and then nodded. 'Broken Ridge is about three hours,' said the first man. 'Not much of a place, but it's all there is until you get to Kernville. That's about two days on from Broken Ridge. Kernville calls itself a city. If half a dozen streets, a lumber mill an' a railroad station make a city, then I guess that's what it is.'

'As long as I can purchase a few supplies somewhere, that's all that matters,' said Caleb. Ephram Barnes returned, followed closely by a small, thin, timid looking woman, barely out of her teens, carrying a bowl. 'Ah, I see my meal has arrived. I thank you, gentlemen.' The woman placed the bowl on one of only two tables and nodded slightly at Caleb.

'That'll be one dollar,' said Ephram from behind the counter. 'There's coffee if you want it. Ten cents a mug, or you can have anythin' from behind the bar.'

'Coffee sounds perfect,' said Caleb, taking some coins from his pocket and handing two of them to the woman. She dutifully handed the money to Ephram. For a moment she stood in the doorway looking almost pleadingly at Caleb. The look of pain and despair in her face was brief, but it had been there, there was no mistaking that fact. When she returned with the coffee, she took great pains to avoid his eyes.

Caleb ate his stew and found it somewhat wanting in some way, but at least it was hot. The look on the woman's face troubled him for a few moments but eventually he dismissed it, not wishing to get himself embroiled in something which was not his concern. He had left the trading post without any trouble from the two men, although he would not have been surprised had they tried to cause difficulties.

Caleb studied the posters again and decided that whoever had drawn the pictures had done so from third- or fourth-hand descriptions rather than knowledge. As a means of identification the drawings were almost useless, but he was quite convinced that the two men he had encountered at the trading post were the two outlaws depicted. He had not taken much notice of it at the time, but when the one man had walked away from the counter he had walked with a definite limp.

'And why would a preacher be interested in posters of outlaws?' a voice suddenly asked behind

Caleb. He turned to face a rather dirty, unshaven man who, going by the badge pinned to his shirt, was the local sheriff.

'At least you recognized the fact that I am a man of God,' said Caleb. 'Too many people seem to assume I have stolen these clothes. As for my interest, even such as I have to make a living. I choose to make mine by bringing men such as these to justice. The Reverend Caleb Black, at your service.'

'You're a bounty hunter?' queried the sheriff. 'Hell, Reveren', I wouldn't let that get out, not round here. You bein' a black man is bad enough, but bein' a bounty hunter as well can only make matters worse for you, 'specially if them two find out. The last bounty hunter through here never made it past Boot Hill. The name suits you though. Matt McCauly, I'm the sheriff round here.'

'Pleased to meet you, Mr McCauly,' said Caleb. 'Does the fact that I am an ordained preacher help me in any way? I see that there is a church in town, so I take it this is a Christian community.'

'I guess you bein' a preacher might help,' said the sheriff. 'Sure, there's a church. It's been a few months since it was used proper though. The last preacher was the Reverend Sam Boulton but he went an' died right in the middle of a weddin' ceremony about three months ago. He'd just reached the part where he pronounces the couple man an' wife when he just dropped dead. They still ain't sure if they're legally married or not.'

'Then I shall be quite happy to correct the situation,' said Caleb. 'Under the circumstances I think that even the colour of my skin will present no problem.'

'Guess not,' shrugged the sheriff. 'I'll ask 'em. What brings a man like you to these parts anyhow, Reveren'?'

'Being a bounty hunter also means that I have to keep moving in order to find more clients,' said Caleb. 'Don't worry, I won't stay any longer than is necessary.'

'I seen you lookin' at the flyers of Parker an' Smith,' continued the sheriff. 'I look at money like that an' even consider handin' in my badge an' takin' up bounty huntin' myself. I can see why you do it, that kind of money is very temptin'.'

'All the more tempting when you know where they are,' replied Caleb.

To his surprise the sheriff simply laughed. 'Every man, woman an' child in these parts knows where they are,' he said. 'Knowin' where they are is one thing, doin' somethin' about it is another. There's three women who are widders an' five kids without a pa in town on account of their men knew where Parker an' Smith were an' reckoned that two thousand dollars was worth the risk.'

'If you know where they are,' said Caleb, 'why haven't you, as sheriff, done something about it?'

'Reveren',' sighed the sheriff. 'I've given myself another two years in this job. By that time I should have enough money saved to buy a few acres of my own. My wife would like it fine if I was to live long enough to do just that.'

'In the meantime those men are free to come and go as they please?' said Caleb. 'That seems a strange way to run a town to me.'

'Yup!' agreed the sheriff. 'That's just how it is though. Parker an' Smith don't bother us an' we don't bother them. Every so often a lawman turns up, usually a deputy marshal, all full of himself an' sayin' just how he's goin' to rid the territory of scum like them. So far though, they've all left empty-handed.'

'And just how does Ephram Barnes fit into all this?' asked Caleb.

'Ephram!' said the sheriff. 'Ephram don't fit in nowhere. That's mostly his own fault though, he won't make the effort to mix. Sure, the fact that his pa was a runaway slave an' his ma a woman no better'n any of the Barnes women are – or were, don't help none. The Barnes clan all moved out more'n ten years ago, all except Ephram that is, even though he warn't much more'n a kid at the time. Seems that even they didn't want anythin' to do with Ephram. Nobody knows where they went, or why, an' nobody don't care either.'

'Well I saw Parker an' Smith out at his place,' explained Caleb. 'When I arrived they seemed to be discussin' business of some sort.'

'Probably talkin' about new ways to take that woman of his,' sneered the sheriff. 'It's common knowledge that he shares her out with anyone he has a mind to an' forces her to take part in what folk round here call orgies. Funny woman too. Nobody's quite sure just where she came from. They reckon she's about ten years younger'n he is, not long out of pigtails. It's even rumoured that he bought her from some passin' Indians. Nobody knows where the Indians got her from an' nobody don't care either.'

'That might explain something,' said Caleb, recalling the look in her eyes. 'Don't the people of Broken Ridge care at all what happens to her?'

'No, sir,' said the sheriff, quite firmly. 'Mind, that could be because some folk wouldn't want anyone lookin' too closely into their own lives.' He gave a dirty laugh. 'It's a job keepin' up with just who is beddin' who round here sometimes.'

'That's nothing unusual,' said Caleb. 'Since it is obvious that men of my colour are not very welcome in these parts, I take it that means I might have difficulty in finding a bed? I have been travelling for more than a week and I really would appreciate a comfortable bed for a few days.'

'I wouldn't say that,' replied the sheriff. 'Mind, you ain't got much of a choice. The only place in town is the saloon. They got three or four rooms they rent out. You can try there I suppose. They had a black feller stayin' there about a year ago. If you'd been an Indian though you definitely wouldn't find a place to sleep.'

'Perhaps it's as well that I'm not a black Indian,' said Caleb with a broad grin. 'Thanks, Sheriff, I'll give it a try.'

As expected, the owner of the saloon looked askance when Caleb asked for a room. At first he thought he was going to be refused but then the owner, Ted Fox, asked if he was a preacher and, rather reluctantly, agreed to let a room when Caleb confirmed that he was.

Having checked in and since there were still a couple of hours until sunset, Caleb stabled his horse, removed his rifle from the saddle holster and then went into the only general store in town where he purchased a few, necessary, items. There was certainly no reluctance on the part of the store owner to accept his money. He asked if there was anywhere he could get something to eat and was informed that the only place was back at the saloon.

On his way back to the saloon, he was met by the sheriff who, true to his word, had asked the young couple who were in doubt as to the legality of their marriage whether or not they wanted Caleb to perform another ceremony.

'Looks like you got yourself some customers, Reveren',' said Sheriff McCauly. 'Most folk round here is God-fearin' folk an' even a black preacher is acceptable sometimes.'

'I'm pleased to hear it,' said Caleb. 'I am also pleased to hear that most folk are believers. Quite why they should be referred to as God-fearing though is something that has always eluded me.'

'Just an expression I guess,' shrugged the sheriff. 'I'll send 'em along to see you. There's a few others who'd like to talk to you as well. Seems that their consciences are botherin' 'em, they ain't been to church proper since Sam Boulton died. I took the liberty of tellin' 'em where you could be found. Oh, there's just one thing, Reveren',' continued the sheriff, 'I hear you checked in to the saloon. I don't know if you is a drinkin' man or not, it don't concern me but, God-fearin' folk or not, it wouldn't be wise to be seen in the bar. Oh, an' one more thing. Folk in these parts ain't used to their preachers wearin' a gun. You'd be doin' yourself a favour if you left it in your room along with that rifle.'

'I have been known to imbibe the demon liquor,' said Caleb, laughing lightly.

'If that means you like drink, I wouldn't recommend it,' warned the sheriff. 'You just keep yourself to yourself an' there shouldn't be too much bother.'

Caleb nodded and returned to the saloon where he ordered a meal. He was not surprised when Ted Fox insisted that it be served in his room. For the sake of peace and quiet, Caleb was ready, if rather reluctant, to agree. The food proved to be very good and quite cheap. About half an hour after he had eaten there was a somewhat timid knock on the door.

'Evenin' Reveren',' said a nervous young man with an even more nervous young woman firmly attached to his arm when Caleb opened the door. 'Mick Lewis. This is my ... er ... my wife, Mary. Leastways we think we are married. That's what we've come to see you about. Mr McCauly told us you were a preacher. . . .'

'Come in,' said Caleb, trying to smile reassuringly. 'Mr McCauly told me what happened. I think we can sort it out.'

'Are you really a proper minister?' asked Mary, nervously.

'As proper and regular as they come,' assured Caleb. 'I do have papers which prove that I am. I carry them because it is a question I am often asked.'

'Mary don't mean no offence, Reveren',' the young man muttered. 'It's just that we ain't never come across a black minister before.'

'There are not too many of us about in this part of the world,' admitted Caleb. 'Please, sit down. All I can offer you is the bed, I am afraid. Mr Fox does not appear too keen to have me in his bar.'

The young couple looked at each other nervously but took up Caleb's offer. The young man coughed and clutched at his hat. 'Did Mr McCauly tell you what happened to the Reverend Boulton?' he asked.

Caleb nodded. 'Well, sir, the thing is we don't know if we're really married or not. Some folk reckon we are but some folk reckon we ain't. The important thing as far as Mary is concerned, is that her folk are among those who reckon we ain't married. They've even tried talkin' her into leavin' me until we can get wed proper. Only trouble with that is there ain't been another preacher through here until you.'

'I refused to leave him, of course,' said Mary. 'I just couldn't do that. I mean, it isn't as if it was Mick's fault. The wedding was almost over, all Mr Boulton had to do was pronounce us man and wife. My folk insist that because he never got that far it means we aren't married. My grandmother – she's very religious – even says it was a sign from God that me and Mick should never get married.'

Caleb smiled and thought for a moment. 'In a way, I suppose that since you were never actually pronounced man and wife, it does mean that you are not really married in the eyes of the church. I wouldn't like to guess as to what the legal situation is. I've never heard of it happening before. However, do not despair. As an ordained minister I have the power and authority to correct the situation. I can perform the ceremony tomorrow if you like. Why didn't you go into the next town, Kernville I believe it's called? They surely have a minister.'

'The last we heard the only minister they had was a Catholic,' said Mary. 'Neither of us are Catholics and I wouldn't feel right being married by a Catholic priest, even supposing he would do it. You're not Catholic are you?' Caleb shook his head. 'Then tomorrow would be perfect.'

'Yes, sir,' enthused Mick. 'Tomorrow would suit us

fine. It is Saturday, so it shouldn't be too hard gettin' our respective folks together.'

'Including grandmother?' said Caleb, laughing.

'Includin' her,' said Mary. 'If what I've heard is right, you'll be meetin' her before then. She sort of appointed herself leader of most of the women round here. Word got round almost as soon as you came into town that you were a minister. She's bringin' some of the other women an' a couple of tame men along to see you.'

'I shall look forward to it,' said Caleb. 'From your description of her she seems a formidable woman.'

'She's used to havin' her own way,' said Mick. 'She ain't really forgiven me for takin' Mary, she never did like me.'

Caleb was standing by the window and looked down on to the street. In the dim light he could see a group of six or seven people, mainly women, striding purposefully along the boardwalk on the opposite side of the street. They stopped opposite the saloon and seemed to talk among themselves. Caleb guessed that the thought of entering a den of inquity such as a saloon was something they found hard to stomach. Eventually one of the men was dispatched across the street.

'She's here,' he said to Mary and Mick. 'What's her name?'

'Higgins, Maud Higgins. Don't ever use her given name though, she's Mrs Higgins to everyone except her two closest friends,' replied Mary, going to the window. She looked out and laughed. 'I thought as much. Not even a minister of the church could make her enter a place like this. She'll probably send for you to talk outside.'

'There's a man on his way up,' said Caleb. 'You'd better go out the back way if you don't want her to know you've been in here. I assume that there is a back way out.' There was a knock at the door. 'Too late,' he said. 'Her messenger is here.' He opened the door to reveal a small, fat man, dressed in a neat, tweed suit.

The man seemed quite surprised to see Mary and Mick, but he did not say anything, although it was plain that he disapproved. Mary laughed, suddenly appearing very happy.

'Good evening, Mr Crabtree,' she said as she pushed past. 'I do hope you will be at my wedding in the morning.' Mr Crabtree seemed lost for words. Mary turned and smiled at Caleb. 'Until tomorrow morning, Reverend,' she said. 'Shall we say ten o'clock at the church?'

'Ten o'clock,' confirmed Caleb.

Mary and Mick disappeared, leaving Mr Crabtree alternately gaping after them and at Caleb. It was not until Caleb asked what he wanted that his mouth closed and he looked at the preacher.

'Mr Black?' he asked. 'The Reverend Black?' Caleb nodded. 'Pardon me, but I was not expecting . . . I didn't realize. . . .'

'That the Reverend Caleb Black was a negro?' said Caleb with a laugh. 'I would have thought whoever told you I was here would also have mentioned the colour of my skin.'

'I . . . we . . . we heard that a minister had arrived in town,' faltered Mr Crabtree. 'We also thought we heard that your name was Black, not that you were. . . . It was just that none of us thought that. . . .'

'An understandable mistake,' said Caleb in an attempt to put the man at his ease. 'However, I am a negro – and proud of that fact – and I am also an ordained minister. I take it you have come to see me in my capacity as a minister, just as the young couple you saw leaving did. I am to perform another wedding ceremony for them at ten o'clock in the morning. Apparently there is some doubt about their original marriage. Now, what can I do for you, Mr Crabtree?'

'Yes . . . well . . .' faltered Mr Crabtree again. 'I was sent to . . . I'm sorry, Reverend, I really don't know what to say. I think perhaps that I had better go and consult with my people again.'

'You do that,' said Caleb. 'I shall wait here.'

Mr Crabtree quickly left the room and Caleb waited by the window. Eventually the little man crossed the street and there followed a hasty conference. All the members of the group looked up at the window, saw Caleb and there followed another hasty conference. Eventually Mr Crabtree was once again dispatched in the direction of the saloon. Caleb heard him walk along the corridor and opened the door.

'I have consulted with my people,' croaked Mr Crabtree. 'They were as surprised as I was but, under the circumstances Mrs Higgins thinks that at least we should talk to you. Since none of the ladies wish to set foot in this place, I have been instructed to ask if you would be kind enough to meet elsewhere. The only other suitable place is the church. Mrs Higgins suggests that we meet there in ten minutes.'

'I shall be there,' promised Caleb.

Ten minutes later Caleb entered the church,

surprised to discover that it was still in very good repair. Six rather large women and two equally rotund men, including Mr Crabtree, were standing in a semicircle opposite the main door.

'The Reverend Caleb Black,' said Mr Crabtree by way of introduction. 'Reverend, may I present my colleagues. . . .' He started by introducing Mrs Higgins first and this was the only name Caleb could remember. It was noticeable that none of them offered to shake his hand.

'You claim to be a minister,' boomed Mrs Higgins when the introductions had been completed. 'Anyone can make such claims. Have you got any proof?' Caleb had been expecting this and produced some papers which he handed to her. 'These could apply to anyone,' she said after she had briefly scanned them. 'It is quite possible that you stole these papers along with your clothes from the real Reverend Black.'

'Ma'am,' sighed Caleb. 'If you cannot believe what your eyes tell you, then there is nothing I can do for you. Good evening to you all.' He recovered the papers and turned to leave.

'Just a moment, Mr Black,' ordered Mrs Higgins. 'I did not say that I disbelieved you. I have to be sure, that is all.'

'In the absence of any further evidence,' said Caleb, 'and your obvious hostility which is more to do with the colour of my skin than proof of my qualifications, I fear there is little I can do for you.'

Mrs Higgins was plainly unused to being addressed in such a way and for a moment she was lost for words. Caleb once again made a move towards the door. 'I hear that you have agreed to conduct a wedding ceremony for my granddaughter,' she suddenly said. 'I would have you know that I am against such a thing. What happened with the Reverend Boulton was plainly a sign from God that the marriage was not to be.'

Caleb turned to face her and smiled. 'My information is that the Reverend Boulton was in his eighties. In my opinion it was not so much a sign from the Lord, more a sign from his body that it had had enough.'

'Yes, well, perhaps so,' muttered Mrs Higgins in apparent agreement. 'It is a fact that he had had two heart attacks shortly before he died. However, that does not alter my mind. I am against the marriage of my granddaughter and Mr Lewis. I have my reasons which need not concern you.'

'Your reasons are your own,' said Caleb. 'As far as I am concerned it is what your granddaughter and Mr Lewis think which is important. I shall conduct the ceremony tomorrow morning at ten o'clock as arranged. I would imagine that you are all welcome to attend, even you, Mrs Higgins.'

Mr Crabtree coughed and spoke. 'I think that family matters need not concern the minister,' he said. 'I for one believe that he is what he claims to be. I know we all were surprised to discover his . . . er. . . .'

'Colour!' said Caleb. 'I make no apologies for the colour of my skin.'

'Very well, Reverend,' said Mrs Crabtree. 'I must admit that I do believe that you are what you claim to be. Are we all agreed?' She scanned the others with a look which defied anyone to disagree. 'Please come back, Mr Black. We wish to discuss other

matters.' As far as Caleb was concerned that meant
that Mrs Higgins wanted to discuss other matters
and the agreement of the others was a foregone
conclusion.

'I am always ready to talk,' said Caleb. 'What can I
do for you?'

Mrs Higgins cleared her throat, obviously still
swallowing her pride at having to deal on equal
terms with a negro. 'We have been unable to attend
church in the normal way since the unfortunate
death of the Reverend Boulton,' she said. 'Don't
misunderstand, we meet every Sunday morning in
this building and give thanks to the Lord. However,
that is not the same thing as having a proper service
conducted by a proper minister. I think I speak for
all here and probably everyone else in town. We
would appreciate it if you would conduct a service of
worship for us.' There was a murmur of agreement.

'Very well, Mrs Higgins,' said Caleb. 'I do not have
any other engagements. I agree.' There was a sigh of
relief from all except Mrs Higgins who glared defiantly at Caleb. 'As for the wedding ceremony, I
suggest you sort that out with your granddaughter.
In the meantime I shall be here at ten o'clock in the
morning as agreed.'

'We shall see,' snorted Mrs Higgins. 'Since it
would appear that she and Mr Lewis are not
married, she still has time to change her mind and
marry Aaron Walters. Now, one more thing. As a
man of the church it is most unseemly for you to stay
at the saloon. That is a place of devil worship, the
abode of the sin and loose women. There are rooms
attached to the church where the Reverend Boulton
used to live. You will stay there. Mrs Day . . .' She

indicated a woman on the end of the line. 'Mrs Day will provide you with food, bedding and anything else you require, just as she did for Mr Boulton.' Mrs Day nodded her readiness to provide such a service.

'I thank you,' said Caleb. 'I must admit that I would prefer somewhere other than the saloon.'

'Then it is settled!' she pronounced. 'Mrs Day lives in the house directly across the street. You will collect your belongings and she will help you move in.'

Caleb grinned. Apparently that was it. Everything had been discussed and settled – at least as far as Mrs Higgins was concerned.

TWO

Shortly after the meeting in the church, Caleb collected his belongings from the saloon and apologized to Ted Fox for leaving at such short notice. It seemed that news of Caleb's confrontation with Mrs Higgins had spread throughout the town. In fact Ted seemed almost relieved that Caleb would no longer be under his roof.

Mrs Day appeared quite surprised at just how little luggage or belongings Caleb had, but she did not make any comment. She fussed around making up a clean bed in what she called 'The Vicarage' – in reality a lean-to building at the side of the church consisting of a bedroom, a sitting room, small kitchen and other usual offices. Water was obtained from a pump just outside the door. Even though Caleb told her that he had already eaten that night, she insisted that she bring food across. Caleb had to admit that it tasted superb.

'The Reverend Boulton ate all his meals in my house,' she said, smiling coyly. 'My husband died many years ago.' Caleb guessed that it was not only meals which the Reverend Sam Boulton had in her house. 'I think perhaps it might be better though if I brought them across to you, don't you think?'

'Whatever you think right and proper,' said Caleb.

'I cook breakfast for seven o'clock,' she continued. 'Is there anything I should know, I mean, is there anything you don't eat for any reason?'

'You cook it, I'll eat it, Mrs Day,' assured Caleb. She appeared quite happy with this.

'Mr Boulton couldn't abide liver or heart,' she explained. 'Not that we see such things all that often, they don't keep.' She once again looked coyly at her new charge. 'If there is anything else you require, you only have to ask. Mrs Higgins and most of the other ladies are very much against strong drink of any kind, but Mr Boulton used to enjoy a glass of whiskey from time to time. I don't mind, men need drink more than women. If you like, I still have half a bottle in the house. Don't ever tell Mrs Higgins about it though, she just wouldn't understand.'

'To be honest, Mrs Day,' said Caleb, 'I too appreciate a glass of good whiskey occasionally. Don't worry, I won't breathe a word to Maud Higgins.'

'Mr Black!' gasped Mrs Day in mock horror. 'Don't ever let her hear you use her Christian name. I've known her for more than thirty years and I am still not allowed to call her that. I don't mind anyone using my given name though. You can do so if you wish. My name is Frances.' Once again she smiled coyly.

'Thank you, Frances,' said Caleb. 'I have the feeling that we will get along just fine. I thank you for all you have done so far. I shall expect you at seven in the morning.'

She seemed almost disappointed and looked at the floor. 'I shall bring the whiskey across.' She looked up and held his gaze for a moment. 'Will ham and eggs be all right?'

'Ham and eggs would be perfect,' said Caleb.

'I'll go and fetch the whiskey,' she croaked.

Ten o'clock the following morning found Caleb, wearing a clean shirt and coat – he always carried a spare set of clothes in his bag – facing Mick and Mary in front of the altar. He was quite surprised to find the church quite full and even Mrs Higgins had turned up, looking anything but happy. However, despite the fact that she would have dearly loved to find an objection to the marriage of her grand-daughter and Mick Lewis, she remained quiet. The service was carried out without a hitch and when he eventually pronounced Mick and Mary man and wife, everyone breathed a great sigh of relief – all except Mrs Higgins and Mary's parents. The marriage was duly recorded in the parish register, something Caleb had been rather surprised to find.

After the ceremony, when most people had departed, Caleb called the couple to one side and asked if there had been any trouble with Mary's parents or her grandmother. He was actually quite surprised that there had been no objections or trouble.

'They tried to make me change my mind,' said Mary. 'In the end I simply walked out and left them to it. I was surprised to see my grandmother here this morning. She had said that she wouldn't come.'

'She told me she wanted you to marry someone called Aaron Walters,' said Caleb.

'Mr Black!' said Mary, laughing. 'Aaron Walters is old enough to be my father. It's true that he's probably the richest man in the territory and has never made any secret of the fact that he wanted to marry me. What he really wants is a housekeeper or someone a lot younger than himself he can show off, not a bride. He and my grandmother tried everything to make me choose him.'

'Was that what your parents wanted as well?' asked Caleb.

'No, although they wouldn't have stopped me,' said Mary. 'They just thought that Mick was not good enough. Have you ever heard of the Barnes clan?' Caleb nodded. 'Well, Mick is one of them. Along with Ephram, they are all that are left of them. Ephram is a Barnes directly, but Mick is only a Barnes because his grandmother was one of the Barnes cousins.'

'Far enough removed,' said Caleb.

'People in these parts have long and bitter memories,' said Mick. 'Barnes is a name which does not go down well. Even anyone remotely related is fair game as far as some folk are concerned. It's true that while they lived in these parts they were nothing but trouble.'

'But your name is Lewis,' said Caleb. 'Perhaps memories are already fading.'

'With most folk, that is the case,' said Mick. 'It's something I can live with.'

With the wedding over and done with, Caleb's thoughts once more turned to the question of the outlaws Parker and Smith. He was quite determined to collect the $2,000 dollars reward. With that in mind he went to see Sheriff McCauly.

'Frankly,' said the sheriff, 'I wouldn't take bets on you bringin' 'em in. They're liable to kill you as soon as look at you. If you do manage it – just supposin' that is – I suggest that you take 'em to Kernville. They'd have to go there anyhow. We just don't have the means of payin' out rewards like that here in Broken Ridge.'

'In other words you don't want the hassle,' said Caleb.

'Somethin' like that,' admitted the sheriff. 'I ain't too proud to admit that I just wouldn't want to chance holdin' 'em here. I'm gettin' old an' I'd like fine to get to be a whole lot older.'

'Don't worry,' said Caleb, 'I'll make sure you don't dirty your hands.'

He left the sheriff's office still without any clear plan in mind. The logical thing to do would be to ride out to Ephram Barnes's trading post and take them. He was convinced that he was quite capable of doing just that, he only wished that Sheriff Matt McCauly would be more helpful.

In the street, Caleb discovered that people now appeared more ready to acknowledge him. Ladies bowed their heads slightly and most men even raised or touched their hats. It seemed that everyone knew that he was to conduct the first regular service in the church the following day. Bearing this in mind, Caleb decided to postpone his visit to the trading post for another day. He felt that there was no great urgency, he did not believe that Parker and Smith would suddenly decide to run. It seemed that the law was on their side. Perhaps not actively, but certainly passively.

The remainder of that day passed without incident and Frances Day appeared very happy now that she once again had a minister to look after. She fed Caleb well, possibly too well. Caleb had to admit that he could quite easily get accustomed to the easy living. Mrs Day did say that it would be nice to have a full time minister in town again, but she also added that she did not believe that Maud Higgins would stand for it in Caleb's case.

'I think she'd be happy to put up with you until a white minister comes along,' she tried to explain. 'The trouble is that she is from an old, southern, slave-owning family and she still thinks of negros as little better than slaves. You know, all right and to be tolerated provided they remember their place. Were you a slave, Reverend?'

'No,' said Caleb. 'I was born a free man. My mother and father were slaves though. Perhaps it might interest Mrs Higgins to know that I was also an officer on the Union side during the war. I was a lieutenant.'

'I don't think she'd be too impressed,' said Mrs Day. 'She was an ardent Confederate and still is.'

Caleb smiled to himself and sighed. It appeared that everything was against him ever becoming acceptable to Maud Higgins.

As he had been advised, Caleb had not worn his guns. However, he did find Mrs Day looking at them in his bedroom. Her reaction was one of confusion. She claimed that she had been cleaning and had 'accidentally' found them. He did not tell her that he was a bounty hunter and explained his possession of the guns away by claiming that they were simply for his protection.

'Since I travel widely,' he said, 'I meet many different types of people. Most are good but some are bad, very bad. They would not think twice about murdering even a minister. In fact some would take delight in doing just that. Even a man of God sometimes needs something more substantial than prayer to protect himself.'

'Mr Boulton did not have a gun,' she pointed out. 'He always said that owning a gun and being a man of God did not go together.'

'If I had a permanent parish I might feel the same,' said Caleb. 'For the moment though, Frances, I would appreciate it if you did not tell anyone.'

'It certainly would not do for Maud Higgins to find out,' she said. 'I think you can rely on me, Reverend.' She brushed past him very closely on her way out of the room.

Caleb stood outside the door to the church, greeting worshippers as they arrived. Mrs Maud Higgins and her entourage had been among the first, claiming as if by right, the front pews. It appeared that almost everyone in Broken Ridge and the outlying farms had turned up. He suspected that those from the farms in the territory had turned out mainly out of curiosity and even Frances Day told him that a good many of them had not set foot inside the church for many years. Caleb was just about to join the congregation when he saw a buckboard draw up on the opposite side of the street.

There was nothing unusual in a buckboard, there had been many others bringing in farmers and their families. The difference was that this one carried Ephram Barnes and the young woman. After a few moments' hesitation, the young woman climbed off the wagon and headed for the church. Ephram Barnes looked at Caleb for a few moments and then whipped his horse into action and the buckboard disappeared. Apparently Ephram was not joining them. Caleb was not at all surprised.

'Welcome,' said Caleb. 'I had not expected to see you.'

'Ephram had some business near town,' she said. 'He agreed that I could go to church if I wanted. It's been a long time since I was allowed to come. I hope you don't mind.'

'All are welcome in the House of the Lord,' declared Caleb. 'The church is full, you might have to stand throughout. Don't worry, I'll try not to keep you standing too long.'

Among Frances Day's attributes, Caleb discovered that she was also the organist. He was never quite certain if the small bellows organ required attention or if Frances Day was rather rusty. Apart from the occasional discordant note from the ancient organ, the service went very well, at least that was the general opinion of the majority and even Mrs Higgins congratulated Caleb. She did admit that she had had misgivings, doubting that Caleb would be up to it. She even admitted that she had expected him to back out at the last moment.

'At least you seem to know your job,' she said. 'It was just a pity that Mrs Day was not quite up to the occasion. I am afraid that we have little choice, however; she is the only person for miles around who can play the organ. I suppose you will be moving on now?'

'I might stay a day or so,' said Caleb. 'I do not

have any particular plans or destination in mind.'

'You are most welcome, of course,' she replied, somewhat frostily. 'It certainly makes a change to have a minister.'

Caleb must have shaken hands with almost everyone, his fingers and wrist were quite painful when the last worshipper had left. Almost gratefully he turned back into the church, fully intending to relax for a time with a glass of Frances Day's whiskey. Frances Day herself was busy cleaning between the rows of pews, complaining to herself and anyone who might hear about how dirty and inconsiderate some people were and the mess they left behind. As he crossed the aisle, a movement in the shadows caught his attention. Ephram Barnes's woman slowly showed herself.

'Can I talk to you?' she whispered, glancing nervously at Frances Day. It seemed that Mrs Day was so engrossed in her cleaning that she had not seen or heard anything. Caleb did not answer but guided the woman through a door into his private quarters.

'You seem very troubled,' said Caleb as he closed the door. 'I thought so when I first saw you. What can I do for you?'

'I . . . I don't know that there is anything you can do for me,' she whispered. 'It's just that. . . . It's just that I don't know who else I can turn to.'

'Ephram?' asked Caleb, indicating a chair. She nodded as she sat down. 'If what I hear is correct, he treats you pretty badly. What is your name? I have to call you something.'

'I suppose it's no more than I deserve,' she choked. 'My Indian name translates as She Who Makes Trouble. I was old enough when the Indians took me to remember my given name. It's Esther. As a young girl, my parents were killed by Indians and I was taken to live with them. I think I was about six years old at the time, I'm not too certain. I was considered trouble by my adopted parents. I know I was, I simply couldn't forget that they had killed my parents. I still remember seeing my mother being scalped. When I was older none of the young bucks wanted to marry me and so eventually I was sold to Ephram.'

'Why stay with him if he ill-treats you?' asked Caleb.

'I've tried running away,' she sighed. 'I shall probably try it again. He always finds me though, drags me back and gives me a good beating. He always reminds me that he paid for me with good whiskey and guns.'

'I hear that he also allows other men to. . . .'

'I hear that as well,' she smiled, weakly. 'That's just the people of Broken Ridge lettin' their imaginations run riot. He beats me if I so much as look at another man. He certainly has never allowed any other man to take me. He'd go berserk if he knew I was in your room – alone.'

'Then perhaps you had better leave before he finds out,' suggested Caleb.

'He won't be back just yet,' she said. 'He's gone out to see Jed Cowling. He lives about three hours away. Jed owes him some money and he's determined to get it and when Ephram is determined, nothing will shake him off. We had to wait just in case Jed had come into town, but he hadn't.'

'So what can I do for you?' he asked.

'Nothing really,' she sighed. 'I just wanted to talk,

to tell someone what he's like. The trouble is that until you appeared there has been nobody to whom I could talk.' Caleb remained silent, not wishing to interrupt her. 'I don't think I can take many more beatings,' she continued. 'Just lately he's taken to beating me just because he doesn't like the way I look at him. He won't mix with people in town. He believes everyone is against him simply because he's a half-caste and a Barnes. Apart from the occasional passing stranger – such as you – the only other people I ever see are those two horrible men, Parker and Smith.'

'Are they any bother to you?' asked Caleb.

'No, to be fair to them they have never tried anything with me. I often wonder what would happen if I did go with one of them and Ephram found out. The only thing that prevents me is the fear that it wouldn't be them he'd kill, it'd be me.'

'For someone who was raised by Indians, you speak very good English,' said Caleb. 'I've come across girls like you before and most of them have forgotten all the English they ever knew.'

'My adopted mother spoke English,' she explained. 'She made certain that I never forgot. That's just about the only thing I have to thank her for.'

'I understand how you must feel,' said Caleb. 'To be honest though, I don't think there is much I can do to help you.'

'I'm not looking for help,' she sighed. 'It just makes a change to have someone listen.'

'Where are Parker and Smith now?' asked Caleb, thinking about how to capture them.

To his surprise she laughed. 'I believe that the

only reason Ephram allowed me to come into town this morning was because he wanted the money Cowling owed him. It would have meant leaving me alone at the trading post and he wouldn't trust me to be there when he returned.'

'Alone?' queried Caleb.

'Yes, Parker and Smith aren't there,' she said. 'Right now I'd say they were staking out the bank in Kernville.'

'Staking out the bank?' asked Caleb. 'What do you mean?'

She looked at him with a very worried expression. 'I've said too much,' she said. 'They don't know I overheard them talking.' She hesitated a moment and then smiled. 'What the hell – if you'll pardon the expression, Reverend. I think I ought to tell someone.' Once again Caleb remained silent to allow her to continue. 'The three of them were talking about robbing the bank in Kernville. Clubfoot reckoned that the bank would be overflowing with money on Monday. It's the end of the month on Wednesday, that's when the workers at the lumber mill get paid. On top of that there's apparently just been a big cattle sale so he reckons the ranchers will be banking their takings. I don't know if that's right or not, but he seemed to know. Anyway, they didn't know I was listening, I heard everything.'

'If he's right, there *could* be a lot of money in the bank,' said Caleb. 'What else did they say?'

'Clubfoot and Vinny seemed to think that robbing the bank would be easy,' she said. 'Anyway, it was agreed that they should do it. Ephram was to hide them. He was to swear that they were at the trading post the whole time if it was necessary. He even told them that I would back up the story. The money was to be hidden in some caves Ephram knows about not too far away and when they thought it was safe they would divide it up. Ephram was to get five thousand dollars as his share.'

'That's a lot of money,' said Caleb.

'Clubfoot reckoned there'd be at least thirty thousand or even more.'

'Are you sure it would be this Monday?' asked Caleb. In his mind he had already added at least $3,000 to the bounty money of $2,000. Ten per cent was the normal reward for the recovery of stolen money.

'Certain,' she confirmed. 'Do you think I ought to tell Sheriff McCauly?'

'Not unless you want to get yourself murdered,' said Caleb. 'If you'll take my advice you'll just carry on as though you know nothing about it. Agree to whatever Ephram tells you to do but on no account tell anyone else what you have told me.'

'But someone ought to know,' she said.

'I know,' said Caleb, smiling and patting her arm. 'Don't worry, I'll make sure they don't get away with it.'

'But what can you do?' she said. 'You're a minister, not a lawman.'

'I also minister to the law,' said Caleb. 'Now, I think you ought to leave. Mrs Day might come in at any moment and I can't vouch that she will not tell others that you were here.' He guided her to the door and out on to the street. 'Just remember, not a word to anyone.' She nodded weakly, plainly confused, and left. A couple of minutes later Mrs

Day came through from the church carrying a large, pewter plate laden with coins.

'I thought I heard voices,' she said, looking around.

'You probably heard me talking to myself,' explained Caleb. 'I often talk to myself. It's a habit most people who travel alone tend to pick up. Well, Frances, I think the service was well received.'

'That it was,' she said, smiling. 'I've never seen the collection plate so full.' She handed it to Caleb. 'Here, this is yours. The minister always takes the collection, it's the only way he gets paid.'

'I thank you, Frances,' said Caleb, taking the plate. 'I shall count it out over a glass of that fine whiskey.'

'Yes, it was nice to see the church so full,' she said. 'The only trouble is that it makes so much more work. You'd never believe the mess some people leave behind. I even found an odd shoe. How anyone could lose just one shoe I'll never know. I took the liberty of placing it on the table by the door. Someone is sure to come back for it. Lunch will be another hour. Today, Reverend, I think it would be in order for you to come across to my place.'

'An hour,' promised Caleb.

After she had left, Caleb poured himself a large whiskey and idly counted out the money from the collection plate while he thought about what to do about Parker and Smith.

There was obviously no question of going after them that day. He had gathered that Kernville was about two days away which would mean his arrival in the town after the robbery had taken place. He briefly toyed with the idea of informing the authorities in Kernville of the impending attempt on their bank but the thought of possibly losing even the reward money out on Parker and Smith made him change his mind.

He had to assume that the robbery would be successful and that they would indeed return to the trading post. On the assumption that the robbery would take place late in the afternoon or possibly during the night, that would mean at least another two days, more likely three, before they made it back to the trading post. He did not mind the extra few days in Broken Ridge, he appeared to have landed himself with something of a sinecure for the moment. He would make his move against the outlaws on the following Thursday. He had to take the chance that they would not be arrested by pursuers. That was very definitely beyond his control.

He looked down absently at the money now in neat piles and tapped the top of each pile of coins as he counted. 'Nine dollars and twenty-three cents,' he muttered, smiling slightly. 'I guess that isn't too bad for an hour's work. Mrs Day should have my lunch ready soon. I wonder what I'll have for dessert?'

THREE

Over the next couple of days, life proved very relaxing for Caleb, almost too agreeably so. At first he even found himself giving serious consideration to taking up the post of minister on a permanent basis as had been tentatively suggested by various people. He had seldom stayed in one place long enough to make a mark and it seemed that most people in Broken Ridge had very quickly come to accept him and his position. Even the dreaded Maud Higgins appeared to have relaxed her rigid ways somewhat and accepted him outwardly, if grudgingly. However, whilst her public face was one of acceptance, in private she told him her true feelings.

'I have no doubts that you are a good man, Reverend,' Maud said when they were alone. 'However, Broken Ridge is a white, Protestant community. I make no apologies for my attitude towards negroes and you are of course free to accept them or refute them since slavery is a thing of the past. My feelings have nothing to do with you personally, you appear genuine and honest. I have no doubt that Mrs Day has told you that my family

38

was a slave-owning family in South Carolina.' Caleb nodded. 'Again, I make no apologies on their behalf, they were of their time and beliefs, as am I. We treated our slaves well, unlike a good many others. My attitude is not entirely biased against negroes either. I can assure you that if a white, Catholic priest were to attempt to settle here, he would be even more unwelcome than you. There certainly would have been no question of allowing him to conduct any form of service and even if he had attempted to, it is most unlikely that he would have had a congregation. It has been suggested that you be asked to take up the post of minister on a permanent basis. Such an idea is complete nonsense of course.'

'You make your feelings very plain and in a way I admire you for that fact. At least I know where I stand,' said Caleb. 'What would you do if I was asked to take on the post on a regular basis? It has been hinted at by more than one. There are others in Broken Ridge, not just Mrs Maud Higgins.' He raised a hand to stifle her rising objection to using her Christian name. 'If the majority wanted it, I do not believe that even you could stop them. You might have authority but you do not have total control. However, you need have no fears that I would accept such an offer. I do not fit in here, quite apart from you and others who think as you, and I am well aware of that fact. Like you, the others are simply making use of me. Oh, I don't mind, I'm used to it. Not only that, I will admit that there are certain things you do not know about me and I do not believe anyone would approve. I shall explain no further, I believe that you will find out very soon. I promise you I shall save you further embarrassment by leaving here in another week at the most.'

'I'll thank you not to refer to me by my Christian name,' she snorted. 'There are only two people in this territory to whom I extend that privilege. Having made the situation very clear, including admitting there are things not yet known about you, you are, of course, free to perform whatever services may be asked of you – religious services that is. I shall not press you on things which might be best kept to yourself.'

'With respect,' said Caleb, smiling. 'Any non religious services are entirely my own affair. However, it would appear that I have a somewhat full week ahead. Already I have been asked to officiate at a funeral – George Salmond apparently died this morning – and three Christenings have been arranged for tomorrow. It would appear that others have need of me even if you do not.'

'You do have your uses in the short term,' grumbled Mrs Higgins.

Some time later Caleb overheard Mrs Higgins and Frances Day talking – or rather Maud Higgins was lecturing Frances Day – warning her that it had not gone unnoticed that she, Frances Day, appeared to be getting a little too close to the Reverend Caleb Black and reminding her that such a liaison was unthinkable under the circumstances.

Later that day, Caleb once again visited Sheriff Matt McCauly, intent on picking his brains and knowledge of the territory.

'Do you have a map of the territory?' Caleb asked.

'Got one here somewheres,' said Matt. 'What you want it for?'

'I just like to know where I am and where I'm going sometimes,' said Caleb. 'Sometimes there are places which are best avoided. I gather Kernville is a largely Catholic town. I don't think a Protestant minister would be too welcome there even if he is bringing in wanted outlaws. I'd like to see if there is anywhere else I might go when I leave there.'

Matt McCauly rummaged in a drawer and eventually pulled out a crumpled sheet which he then spread across a table. 'You're still determined to go after Parker an' Smith then?' he said. 'You'll be needin' someone to take *your* funeral service I reckon. You might have to rely on Father Ignatius from Kernville. This is it, it's more'n fifteen years old but I guess things ain't changed that much since then. I hear Frances Day has been warned not to be so friendly with you.'

'Broken Ridge seems to have a very efficient telegraph system,' smiled Caleb. 'That happened no more than an hour ago.'

'Some things get round almost as soon as they're said,' said Matt, laughing. 'I also hear that Maud Higgins refuses to allow you to become our regular preacher. There's no knowin' what she'd do or say if she knew you were a bounty hunter.'

'Maud Higgins is entitled to her opinions, as we all are,' replied Caleb, bending over the map, flattening it out with his hands and peering at it. 'It would seem that Maud Higgins is the only person around here who can make a decision on anything. I do not think it would make a great deal of difference if she did know about my other life.' He peered more closely at the map. 'Ah, here we are, Broken Ridge. Where is Kernville?'

'She makes all the decisions on account of she owns almost everythin',' said Matt. 'It's she who pays my wages. Only things she don't own are the saloon, the general store an' the church. Everyone else either works for her or pays rent. That includes most of the farms in the territory. Most of them are mortgaged to her. Only Aaron Walters is reckoned to be richer'n she is an' nobody knows where he got his money from.' He indicated a spot almost due north of Broken Ridge. 'Kernville is right here.'

'I should have guessed it was something like that,' said Caleb. 'I suppose that explains why everyone is scared of her.' He drew his finger along a line between Broken Ridge and Kernville. 'And that's two days away?' he queried. 'It certainly doesn't look that far.'

'If you sprouted wings it'd take you less'n a day,' agreed Matt. 'This map don't show the mountains an' canyons all that well. See this here?' He indicated a long, narrow shaded area. 'That's what they call Smokey Bear Canyon. Kernville is that side, Broken Ridge is this side. Like I say, if'n you could go direct or sprouted wings to fly across the canyon, it'd take less'n a day. Trouble is, Smokey Bear Canyon is somethin' like a thousand feet deep all along here . . .' He drew his finger along most of the shaded area. 'It's almost a mile wide as well. They reckon even mountain goats can't find a foothold on the sides of the canyon an' if they can't climb it then there ain't nobody can climb it. There were some crazy Englishmen here a couple of years ago an' they tried to climb down it. Their bones are still down there somewhere.'

'Is there no way down at all?' asked Caleb. He was

considering the possibility of Parker and Smith making a quick exit directly across the canyon from Kernville.

'There's one sure way down,' said Matt, laughing. 'That's straight over the edge. No, sir, as far as I know the only way is round. It don't matter much which way you go, it's about the same distance to Kernville. Most folk take the eastern route, they reckon it's a bit easier crossin' the river that way, but it don't really matter.'

Caleb studied the map while the sheriff talked to someone who had entered the office. He found Ephram Barnes's trading post and soon worked out that there would be no need for the outlaws to come very close to Broken Ridge and that the shortest route would be via the western end of the canyon.

'Is there a telegraph office in town?' Caleb asked when the sheriff returned. 'I haven't seen one.'

'There was talk about puttin' the telegraph through here some years ago,' said Matt. 'It just never happened though. Nobody ever did find out why not for sure. Some say it was Mrs Higgins who doesn't agree with all these new-fangled ideas. Still, I don't reckon we're missin' much. Nobody in these parts really needs it. If anyone wants to send a message they have to go into Kernville.'

Caleb thought it a pity, he would have liked to have known well in advance if Parker and Smith had been successful or not. It would certainly have helped him to form some sort of plan. The one thing he had established in his own mind, was that if they were to push their horses as fast as they could, it was quite possible that they could make the journey from Kernville to Ephram's trading post in well under twenty-four hours. This he knew for a fact, he had once made a similar journey himself, riding nineteen hours with hardly a stop.

He had long since learned that a two-day journey was thought of in terms of two days of fairly slow travelling, riding no more than nine or ten hours a day with frequent stops. He revised his estimate of when Parker and Smith would show up to sometime in the evening of the next day.

He would have liked to have been at the trading post when the outlaws returned and that was still possible. The next day was Tuesday and he had arranged three christenings for the morning and the funeral of George Salmond for two o'clock in the afternoon. Even allowing for a few delays, he could probably make it to the trading post before Parker and Smith returned. It was, of course, quite possible, since they were wanted outlaws, that they might simply ride on or even take off from Kernville in a different direction. That was something he had to chance, but somehow he thought it unlikely since they appeared to be taking precautions. This, in fact, puzzled Caleb.

'I was thinking about Parker and Smith,' he said to Matt McCauly. 'There's something that doesn't seem right to me. I would have thought someone would have made a real effort to take them in. It seems everyone knows where they are.'

'Some folk have tried,' said Matt. 'I already told you we have the odd deputy marshal wantin' to make a name for himself through here sometimes. There's just one thing though. They is safe enough where they are on account of they ain't in this State. In fact where they are ain't nowhere from what I can gather. The State border is about five miles this side of the tradin' post. Where they are ain't in the Union yet, so Union or Federal laws ain't so easy to enforce. It can be done, but it means lots of work for the lawyers. Usually wanted men are kidnapped an' brought across the border. There's been a few complaints but it seems to work. If you do take 'em you're goin' to have to bring 'em across. The nearest town of any size south of the border is River Bend. Since they ain't wanted there though, there's no reward.'

'That might explain a couple of things,' said Caleb. 'If there's no telegraph, how do you find out what's happening?'

'If it's anythin' really important we get a man from Kernville ridin' in. Other than that we get the stage an' the mail through here twice a week. Wednesdays it comes from Kernville on its way to Reno. Saturdays it comes from Reno through to Kernville.'

There was little else Caleb could do. In fact for the remainder of the day he was fully occupied with the three christenings and the funeral. For these services he was able to add another ten dollars to his income. He could see why priests and ministers always appeared quite well off. An income of something between ten and twenty dollars a week was well above the average the normal man might expect to earn. Even if the incumbent was expected to pay for his own keep and food, it was still a good income.

It was almost four o'clock before Caleb was able to leave Broken Ridge and ride out to the trading post. He told Mrs Day where he was going but not why and asked her not to tell Mrs Higgins. It was not that he was worried about Maud Higgins, he simply thought it best if she did not know. Mrs Day agreed, stating vehemently that what she, Frances Day, did or what the minister did, was no concern of Maud Higgins, even if she did own almost everything and even if the minister had taken his guns with him. She did not press him on just why he was going or why he needed to be armed.

It was well past nightfall when Caleb eventually arrived within sight of the trading post. There were a couple of oil lamps burning, but there did not appear to be any sign of life. He finally settled himself amongst a clump of trees, his horse tethered out of sight, and resigned himself to a long wait.

During the time he was waiting, he did see the woman, Esther, go to the water-pump a couple of times and he briefly saw Ephram Barnes peering out of a window. In actual fact, although he had not intended to do so, Caleb fell asleep. He was only made aware of that fact when he was woken by the sound of horses. He glanced at his pocket watch and managed to decipher that the time was just after midnight.

Two rather distressed horses pulled up outside the trading post and immediately Ephram Barnes dashed out. After a brief exchange of excited words and obvious pleasure with themselves on the part of Parker and Smith, they went inside carrying four sacks. The robbery had obviously been a great success. Caleb was quite pleased that his calculations of when they would show up had proved so accurate. It made a change. Usually his calculations and plans had a habit of going wrong.

He was about to make his move against the outlaws and Ephram Barnes when the three of them suddenly reappeared, mounted their horses – Ephram apparently already having one saddled, which Caleb had not seen, at the side of the building and raced off into the night. Caleb cursed and was about to go after them when Esther appeared at the door.

It was quite plain that Caleb had little hope of following the outlaws in the dark and even if he did, the chances of taking them all were remote. He allowed them another few minutes – during which time Esther had returned inside – before leading his horse down to the building where he took it round the back, out of sight.

'Miss Esther!' he called out. 'It's only me, Caleb Black. Can I come in?'

A timid face appeared at the door, clutching an ancient muzzle-loading rifle. She peered at Caleb for a few moments and eventually stood aside to allow him to enter.

'You saw them come back an' then go,' she said. 'You must've done, otherwise you wouldn't dare come anywhere near.'

'I saw them,' admitted Caleb. 'It looks like the robbery was a success.'

'Over thirty-eight thousand dollars according to Clubfoot,' she confirmed. 'They think there's a posse after them, that's why they went off to the caves to hide the money tonight.'

'Do you know where these caves are?' he asked.

'Not exactly,' she said. 'Somewhere's up on Bailey's Ridge. That's about five miles east of here. That's all I know.'

'I'll probably be able to find it, with your help of course,' said Caleb, smiling. 'I shall wait here until they return.'

'Wait here! They'll kill you,' she warned. 'They'll kill anyone who tries to come between them and that money.'

Caleb laughed. 'They might be expecting a posse but they won't be expecting one, lone, minister.' He took out both his pistols and checked them. He laughed again when he saw the surprised look on Esther's face. 'Yes, two guns,' he said. 'I can use both of them as well. I believe I told you that I ministered to the law as well. You might as well know the truth of it, I am also a bounty hunter.'

'A bounty hunter!' she exclaimed. 'Does that mean you're not really a preacher?'

'No, it does not mean that,' he said, replacing the guns. 'I am truly a minister of the church but I am also a bounty hunter. I find it more profitable than saving souls. Take my advice and keep well out of the way when they do come back. There could be a few stray bullets – not mine, theirs. I'd prefer to take Parker and Smith alive. That way they are worth two thousand dollars. I'm not quite sure what the position is if they are dead, but I expect it to be at least one thousand. Your Ephram, as far as I know, isn't worth a thing dead or alive. Then of course there's the reward for returning the bank's money.'

'I hope you manage it,' she said. 'Ephram gave me another good beating today. All I did was drop a bowl of stew. If you do manage it at least I shall be free to go just where I want to.' She sighed and smiled. 'I shall go to San Francisco. I've always wanted to go there ever since I met a feller from there. Ile told me such wonderful tales about how big it is, about how easy it is to make money.'

'I wouldn't believe everything you hear,' said Caleb. 'I went there once, when I was in the army. I didn't think much of the place.'

'I don't care,' she said. 'That's where I'll go.'

'And what will you do for money?' he asked.

Esther smiled and then burst out laughing. 'If all else fails, there's one sure way a girl can earn a living,' she said. 'I don't think it'll come to that though, not for a while at least. You owe me, Reverend. I told you about the bank. Let's say you give me half of what you make. Always supposin' you do make anythin'.'

'And if I get killed?'

'Then things stay the same as they are now,' she said. 'I guess I can take a few more beatings.'

'I suppose you're right,' he conceded. 'I do feel bound to help you. I'll give you one thousand dollars. That's probably more money than you have ever seen in your life.'

'One hell of a lot more,' she admitted. 'Make it two thousand, the amount you earn from Parker and Smith and you have a deal. I'm a girl of simple tastes and fairly easy to please.'

'For the moment all this is pure speculation,' he said. 'You are quite right, I could end up with nothing, not even my life. We'll talk about it when the time arrives and not before. Now, I suggest you take yourself off to bed. Leave the lamps burning, I need to see them when they come into the room.'

'They won't be back for hours,' she said, smiling at Caleb and thrusting out her chest. 'We've got time for a bit of fun.'

'I have other ideas of fun,' he said. 'It's not that you are an unattractive woman, it's just that I don't like to mix work with pleasure. Perhaps some other time.'

'Suit yourself!' she huffed.

She flounced off, leaving Caleb to rearrange the furniture slightly in order to give himself the element of surprise. When he was satisfied he sat opposite the door and waited.

Dawn was just breaking when he heard the horses draw up. A quick look outside confirmed that it was the outlaws and Ephram Barnes and not the posse. Eventually the three of them stomped into the room, Ephram calling for Esther.

'There's no need to disturb her,' said Caleb, moving out of a shadow, both his guns levelled at them. 'Don't even think about it,' he warned as Vinny Smith's hand moved towards his gun. 'I am very accurate with either hand.'

'What the hell is this?' demanded Clubfoot Parker. 'Ain't you that preacher what passed through a few days ago? We heard you'd taken up preachin' in Broken Ridge.'

'The very same,' agreed Caleb. 'Since then I have discovered that you are worth quite a lot of money and since preachers are always looking for money I thought it might be a good idea if I collected the reward.'

'A bounty hunter!' exclaimed Smith. 'I thought there wasn't somethin' quite right about you.'

'Oh, I am a regular preacher,' said Caleb. 'I just find people like you rather more profitable. Now, very slowly, drop your guns. You too, Ephram.' At that moment Esther appeared and looked genuinely surprised. 'Just stay over there,' advised Caleb. 'Now, do as I say. Drop those guns. I might be a man of the church, but I can assure you that I am not above killing anyone if I think it necessary. There have been quite a few who have made that mistake.'

'OK, Mr Preacherman,' sneered Parker. 'Right now you got the drop on us. There's only one place you can take us though an' that's Kernville an' that's a mighty long way.'

'I've taken men like you further,' said Caleb. 'Now, drop those guns, my fingers are getting tired.' They looked at each other and decided that Caleb was not joking. They lowered their gunbelts and waited.

'There's no reward out on me,' said Ephram. 'You ain't got no right on me.'

'These guns say that I have every right,' warned Caleb. 'I think a charge of helping bank robbers will be enough to put you away for a very long time.'

'Bank robbers! What you talkin' about?' grated Parker.

'I'm talking about you robbing the bank in Kernville,' said Caleb.

'How in the hell did you know about that?' demanded Parker. 'We only did that a few hours ago, there ain't no way you could've heard about it. OK, Mr Preacherman, if we robbed the bank, where's the money?'

'You must remember that I have friends in high places,' mocked Caleb. 'The Good Lord knows everything.'

The three of them looked at each other uneasily

for a moment. 'Crap!' rasped Smith. 'I don't believe in shit talk like that.' He glanced at Esther and slowly smiled. 'She told you,' he said. 'That's it, she found out about it an' she told you.' He glared at Ephram. 'Couldn't keep your big mouth shut could you?'

'I never said a word to her,' objected Ephram. 'She must've overheard us talkin'.'

'Whatever the reason, gentlemen,' said Caleb. 'You are now under arrest for the bank robbery in Kernville and also the fact that you, Clubfoot Parker and you, Vincent Smith, are wanted outlaws worth one thousand dollars each.'

'Not in this territory we ain't,' said Parker.

'I realize that,' Caleb nodded in agreement. 'Which is why I have to get you back to Broken Ridge. There you are worth a thousand dollars each. You might be worth even more after that robbery if they know it was you. Esther, pick up their guns and put them on that table. Do you know how to unload them?' She nodded. 'Then do it, it will make them less tempting.' She proceeded to unload the guns. 'Do they know it was you?' he asked.

'Don't know if they know or not,' said Smith. 'We sure didn't go round tellin' anyone who we were.'

'We shall soon find out,' said Caleb. 'I expect there will be a posse out looking for you. Now, Ephram, you take some of that twine you've got over there and tie their hands behind their backs.' Ephram looked at Parker and Smith but did not move. 'Please, Mr Barnes,' said Caleb. 'Do as I say. My finger is becoming very tired and it is difficult to keep it from squeezing this trigger.' A shot suddenly splintered the wood close to Ephram's ear and all three men ducked. 'Dear me,' continued Caleb. 'I just couldn't stop it. The other one is getting just as tired.'

This time Ephram ran to a counter, grabbed some twine and immediately set about tying the hands of Parker and Smith behind their backs. When he had finished, Caleb checked that the bonds were tight enough. He then ordered Ephram to turn round while he tied his hands.

'I believe that will suffice until we reach Broken Ridge,' he said. 'Esther, my horse is out at the back. Please bring it round the front. Are you coming to Broken Ridge with us?'

'There don't seem much point,' she said. 'I wouldn't be much help.'

'Then wait here,' said Caleb. 'I shall return as soon as I can and together we shall look for the money.'

'You'll never find it,' sneered Ephram.

'We shall see,' said Caleb. 'Now, gentlemen, please go outside where I shall help you to mount your horses. Oh, and please remember. These guns are what they call Navy Colts. That means they have longer barrels than normal and have a much greater range. You would not get far.'

FOUR

Caleb, his prisoners and the posse arrived in Broken Ridge at exactly the same time. As Caleb ushered his charges in at one end the town, the posse galloped in at the other end. They met outside Sheriff Matt McCauly's office. The man leading the posse looked at Caleb and his prisoners and immediately reacted by ordering the arrest of them all, including Caleb. They were surrounded by the posse, guns levelled, almost daring Caleb to do something.

Matt McCauly had already emerged from his office and it seemed that the entire population of Broken Ridge was also turning out to see what all the fuss was about. Matt greeted the leader of the posse, plainly well acquainted with him.

'Afternoon, Barney,' said Matt. 'What the hell is goin' on round here? Nobody ever tells me a darned thing.'

'These men are under arrest,' replied Deputy Marshal Barnaby Wells. 'The bank at Kernville was robbed two nights ago an' we know that Parker an' Smith were seen in town just before it happened.

Anyhow, we followed their tracks back towards Broken Ridge.'

'I'll buy that for them two but not Ephram or the Reverend,' said Matt. 'There ain't no way the Reverend here could've been involved. Yesterday afternoon he was buryin' George Salmond.'

'Reverend!' queried Wells. He looked more closely at Caleb. 'Are you tellin' me he's a minister? Since when did a reverend wear a gun?'

'Gun or not, he most certainly is a reverend, young man,' came a voice as Maud Higgins pushed her way through the crowd. 'He is the Reverend Caleb Black. At present he is our minister. If need be I can confirm that he was in town until four o'clock yesterday afternoon which means that it would have been impossible for him to be involved in a bank robbery and then ride back here in time to conduct three christenings and then a funeral in the afternoon. Where he has been since then I do not know, but he has plainly been fully occupied. I think you owe our minister an apology, Mr Wells. He has obviously saved you a lot of time and effort. Not only that, but he seems to have succeeded where the law has constantly failed in bringing these two outlaws to justice.'

The deputy looked stunned. He eventually gulped and nodded, apparently well aware of just who and what he was up against. 'Sure thing, Mrs Higgins,' he said. 'If you say he's your minister then I guess he is an' if you say he was here then I guess he was. There's just one thing wrong with all that though, he's black an' . . .'

'Have you not heard that there was a war recently,' she interrupted. 'Whatever my or your

feelings or allegiances regarding that conflict, it is
now the law that slavery has been abolished and that
all men, regardless of their colour, are equal.'

'Yes, ma'am,' grunted the deputy. 'OK, you're
free to go . . . Reverend. Just one thing. How in the
name of hell did you know these men were wanted
for robbing the bank? Broken Ridge doesn't have
the telegraph.'

'I have access to the highest authority,' said Caleb,
laughing. 'Seriously, I shall be happy to explain. For
the moment though, it is sufficient that my original
reason for arresting them had nothing to do with
the robbery – I learned about that later. I believe
that they are wanted outlaws with a reward of one
thousand dollars each. I wish to make it known that
I stake my claim to that reward.'

'Yeah . . . OK, you made your point,' conceded
the deputy. 'You'll have to sort that out back in
Kernville. In the meantime, Matt,' he said, addressing the sheriff. 'They'll have to be locked up in your
jail. Don't worry, we'll have 'em out of here first
thing in the mornin' an' there'll be at least two men
on guard all the time.'

'Ephram too?' asked Matt. 'He couldn't've had
anythin' to do with the robbery either. I saw him
yesterday afternoon while I was out at the Silvester
farm. There's no way he could've been there.'

'Then just why have you brought him in,
Reverend?' demanded the deputy. 'Don't tell me
there's a price on his head too 'cos I ain't never
heard of one.'

'He is an accomplice,' said Caleb. 'He arranged
for the money to be hidden.'

'He don't know what he's talkin' about,' objected

Ephram. 'Sure, I'll admit I know Parker an' Smith
well enough. There ain't no law against that though.
You know as well as I do that my place ain't in this
State. Neither Parker nor Smith is wanted for
anythin' where I come from. I ain't broken no law.'

'I find that hard to believe,' sneered Deputy
Marshal Wells. 'Anyhow, we can't talk out here, get
them two inside an' locked up. We'll sort this out
over some coffee an' some food. Me an' my boys are
all starvin' hungry. We've had a long, hard ride. Get
some food sent over from the saloon, Matt.'

'You heard what he said,' said Matt, addressing
Ted Fox, the owner of the saloon, who had joined
the crowd. 'I'll see to your bill.'

'Sure thing,' agreed Ted Fox. 'I got beef stew or I
got steak, which is it to be?'

'Make that six steaks an' one stew,' said the deputy
after a brief consultation with his men. 'Big ones an'
don't stint on the vegetables.'

'Reverend,' said Mrs Higgins. 'When you have
finished your business, I would appreciate it if you
would come and see me.'

'I shall be there,' said Caleb, smiling and raising
his hat slightly.

The two outlaws and Ephram Barnes were
marched into the sheriff's office where Parker and
Smith were freed of their bonds and placed in the
only cell. Ephram Barnes was also freed but told to
wait.

'Now, Reverend,' said Deputy Marshal Barnaby
Wells. 'I think you've got some explaining to do,
especially if you want to collect that reward. First
time I ever heard of a minister claimin' a reward
like that though.' He looked down at Caleb's gun

and casually, using the barrel of his rifle, flicked Caleb's long coat to one side to reveal the second pistol. 'I thought so. First time I ever actually seen any man wearin' two guns either, let alone a preacher. Can you use both of 'em? Don't answer that, I reckon you probably can and have done on many occasions. I'd say you were a professional bounty hunter.'

'Well I certainly don't do it so that I can pay for church restoration,' said Caleb.

'Well now I seen everythin', I reckon,' said Wells. 'I'm waitin' for your explanation, Reverend, an' don't try shootin' me no religious crap.'

'Religion is not crap, Mr Deputy,' said Caleb. 'It will be a pleasure. . . .' He went on to explain in minute detail just what had happened since meeting the men out at Ephram's trading post.

'You make it sound so damned easy,' said Wells, shaking his head in apparent disbelief. 'We've been tryin' to get our hands on these two for maybe three years now and not succeeded. Then along comes somebody like you and arrests them just like that. What did everyone else do wrong?'

'Remember I have a powerful ally,' suggested Caleb, laughingly. 'Anything is possible with God's help.'

'If you say so, Mr Black,' grunted Wells. 'And you think that the money is in these caves somewhere? Do you know where these caves are, Matt?'

'Can't say as I do,' said Matt. 'Caves ain't all that uncommon in these parts though. There's quite a few up on Broken Ridge itself so I don't see why they can't be up on Bailey's Ridge. Bailey's Ridge is just an extension of Broken Ridge. Before there were settlers in these parts they reckon the caves were home to the local Indians.'

'And you, Barnes,' said the deputy. 'Do you know of these caves?'

'I heard of 'em,' snarled Ephram.

'You must know them,' sneered the deputy. 'That's where you've hidden the money isn't it?'

'I ain't got the faintest idea what you're talkin' about,' grunted Ephram. 'What money? I sure didn't see none.'

'No? We'll see,' said the deputy. 'Matt, how far is it to these caves?'

'Don't know exactly,' said Matt. 'I don't know exactly where they are. Bailey's Ridge is about four hours. It straddles the border.'

'And it is now just after midday,' said the deputy, looking at his pocket watch. 'That means we could be there before nightfall. You ain't got no deputies have you, Matt?' he continued. 'I'll leave deputy sheriff Jim Lovatt an' three of the others here to look after the prisoners. Jim Lovatt is a deputy sheriff in Kernville,' he explained to Caleb. 'You, me, Matt an' Ephram here are all goin' out to Bailey's Ridge to look for that money.'

'Do I still get my cut?' asked Caleb.

'That's somethin' you'll have to sort out with the bank,' said Wells. 'Don't see why not though. If it is there you can claim it was you who led us to it. I'll back you up on that.'

At that moment the steaks arrived. Caleb was also feeling hungry and took his leave, promising to return in time to go out to Bailey's Ridge. His first call was on Frances Day who seemed to have anticipated that he would be hungry and had also laid on

a large steak. Although it was plain that she was
almost bursting with curiosity, she did not actually
ask her charge what had happened and Caleb only
increased her tension by not volunteering the information. Before he returned to the sheriff's office, he
called on Mrs Higgins, as promised and instructed.

'I must confess that I do not find myself surprised
by the turn of events,' she said. 'I presume you are
what is called, I believe, a bounty hunter? That is
what the people of Broken Ridge are now saying.'
Caleb nodded and smiled. 'Of course I strongly
disapprove, I never did like bounty hunters, not that
I have met many. The few I have encountered have
been dirty and very discourteous. It is, in my opinion, most unbecoming for a minister of any church
to resort to such barbaric methods as hunting men
for money.'

'But it is permissible to hunt men for their souls?'
said Caleb. 'I see little conflict. It is the duty of every
minister, whatever his actual religious persuasion, to
save souls for God. Unfortunately the vast majority
of ministers or priests choose to live and preach
among those already converted. It is so much easier
and probably more profitable. I look upon myself as
a kind of missionary. I have chosen, in addition to
working with the faithful, to extend the Mercy of
Christ to those who have strayed from the path of
righteousness. It is also the duty of every citizen,
men of God included, to bring to justice all those
who have transgressed the civil law. In transgressing
the law of the land, they have certainly transgressed
God's law. I bring men such as Parker and Smith to
the lawful authorities and at the same time I pray for
their salvation. You would be surprised at just how

many of them repent their ways, especially so when they face the prospect of hanging for their crimes. In this way I am serving the Good Lord. The fact that in most cases there happens to be a reward for the capture of those men is incidental but nevertheless most welcome. Even a roving minister of religion such as I needs to eat and pay his way. In fact I rarely see much benefit from the rewards I collect. I usually end up giving most of it away to those in need.'

'A very pretty speech!' snorted Maud Higgins. 'Young man, I have been around a long time. I have seen ministers come and go, good ones and bad ones. I have often despaired of some of them. As you say, they are content to live among and off the converted. Whilst I do not believe a word you have said, it has to he admitted that you do appear to be genuine and sincere in your administration of the church. Actually I can well believe that you do give most of your money away. I must also admit that in collecting rewards you cannot be accused of sponging off others.'

'I thank you for calling me a young man,' said Caleb, smiling. 'I believe that I am not that many years behind you.'

'*All* men are young as far as I am concerned,' she said, also smiling. 'I would imagine that I am at least twenty-five years your senior. Be that as it may,' she continued. 'What I want to make plain is that this little episode has simply reinforced my belief that you are unsuitable for the post of minister in Broken Ridge. I had already sent a petition, before your arrival, asking for a minister to be sent here at the very earliest opportunity. Today I received a reply, brought here from Kernville by Deputy Sheriff Jim Lovatt, stating that a minister will be sent at the end of next month. I gather he is a young man, newly ordained. No doubt he will be quite happy to live among the converted and I have no doubt that we, the converted, shall be only too happy to have him amongst us. In the meantime, Reverend, you are quite welcome to remain here until the new minister arrives. It is the least we can do and general opinion would appear to be in your favour.'

'Most gracious of *you*, I'm sure,' said Caleb with a large amount of irony. 'For the moment though it seems that my services are required elsewhere. The money from the bank robbery has yet to be recovered and I believe I can help. I shall give serious consideration to your offer, Mrs Higgins.'

'Most gracious of *you*, I'm sure,' she responded with equal irony.

Caleb bowed slightly and smiled but said nothing. He realized that there was no way he would ever win a battle of words or wills with Maud Higgins.

Caleb joined Deputy Marshal Barnaby Wells and Sheriff Matt McCauly and half an hour later, along with a grumbling Ephram Barnes and two members of the posse they rode out of town. Word had already spread as to where they were going and what for. There were even suggestions by a few of the less savoury citizens of Broken Ridge that they too might go searching for the money.

Less than four hours later Matt McCauly led them up a steep slope where he called a halt. They looked down on to an even steeper slope with a small river twisting its way along the bottom.

'Now I ain't too sure if this ridge is the border or

that river down there,' he said. 'It's somethin' that don't normally concern me all that much. Anyhow, this is the start of Bailey's Ridge. It goes on for about ten miles an' I reckon the caves could be anywhere.'

'Well?' said Barnaby Wells to Ephram. 'You tell us.'

'Marshal!' sighed Ephram. 'How in the name of hell can I tell you somethin' I don't know?'

'You can start by not pretendin',' said Wells. 'We know Parker and Smith robbed that bank an' we know they rode back here. The Reverend here can also testify to the fact that you rode off with them almost as soon as they came back. I'd say the Reverend's word alone was enough to ensure that you get a long term in prison for what they call aidin' an' abettin'.'

'He's lyin'!' snarled Ephram.

'I think any jury might tend to believe a minister of the church rather than a man like you,' said Matt McCauly.

'On account of my colour?' grunted Ephram. 'Or maybe 'cos my name is Barnes an' we all know what folk in these parts think about anyone with that name.'

'The reverend is also black,' Wells pointed out. 'In fact he's blacker'n you, you're only half black.'

'Well, it don't make no difference,' said Ephram, scowling at Caleb. 'I don't know nothin' about no money nor no robbery an' you can't prove that I do.'

'We'll see,' grunted Wells. 'OK across the border or not, we go down an' start lookin' for caves. Anyhow, we could do with findin' somewhere to rest up for the night.'

When they reached the river, Matt McCauly suddenly swore and pointed back to where they had come from. 'That's a good start,' he said. 'We rode straight past a cave. Knowin' our luck, if we ignored it that'd turn out to be the one where the money is. You carry on, I'll go back an' take a look. I'll catch you up.'

The sheriff rode back up the slope and the others slowly made their way along the river bank. If there were any other caves in the immediate vicinity, they were well hidden. They had travelled about half a mile when Barney Wells stopped and pointed at a short section of vertical rock.

'That looks like a cave up there,' he said. 'Even if it ain't where the money is it looks as good a place as any to rest up.'

Suddenly Caleb swung his rifle to his shoulder and fired; the others immediately drew their guns and looked about for a target, struggling to hold their horses spooked by the shot. 'Well, we have to eat and nobody thought about bringing food did they?' said Caleb casually, replacing his rifle and dismounting. At the same time Matt McCauly raced into view, gun at the ready and demanding to know what was going on. 'I have just shot our dinner,' said Caleb, going across to some shrubs. He bent down and dragged a small deer into view.

'Reverend!' sighed Barney Wells. 'Don't you ever do a damn fool thing like that again. You could easily get yourself killed. You should have warned us.'

'By which time dinner would have been well out of sight,' said Caleb. 'The one thing I have learned about being a travelling man is that when the oppor-

tunity presents itself you have to take it. I assume
there was nothing in that cave, Sheriff?'

'Nothin' I could see,' said Matt. 'It wasn't all that
big.'

'I would imagine that even Parker, Smith and
Ephram here would not be so simple minded as to
leave the money just lying about,' said Caleb. 'They
would make certain it was well hidden, somewhere
dry. They might have buried it even.'

'Not in that cave they wouldn't,' asserted Matt. 'It
was all solid rock, no sign of anyone tryin' to dig an'
there was no loose rock either. You can take it from
me, it wasn't in there.'

'OK,' said Barney. 'We're headin' up there.' He
pointed at the sheer face. 'There looks like there
might be some caves up there. Anyhow, we're restin'
up for the night. Thanks to the reverend, at least we
won't go hungry.'

Caleb and one of the two men from the posse
manhandled the carcass of the deer across Caleb's
horse and Caleb followed them up the slope, leading his horse. They found three caves and immediately Barney Wells dispatched the men from the
posse to search two of them while he and Matt
searched the nearest and largest. Caleb instructed
Ephram to gather wood for a fire while he expertly
skinned and butchered the deer.

'All very interestin',' grunted Matt. 'We're here to
look for stolen money though, not drawing's on
walls.'

'Well there's no sign of it,' said Barney. 'I just
thought you'd be interested, that's all. I hear there's
some folk who make their livin' searchin' old places
like this. I am kinda interested in things like that

myself. How about you, Reverend?'

'I must confess to have very little interest in such things,' admitted Caleb. 'I have heard of people who are though. I believe they are called archaeologists or something. Personally I would have been very surprised if the money had been in a place like this. It is far too obvious, even if very few people come up here. I believe, gentlemen, that we must look for a cave which is well hidden, perhaps with only a very small entrance through which one has to crawl.'

'On the other hand we could make Ephram here show us exactly where it is,' suggested Barney, threateningly fingering the blade of his knife and grinning at Ephram. 'Make things easy for yourself, Barnes,' he said. 'Tell us where it is. Better still, show us.'

'I already told you,' snarled Ephram. 'I don't even know what you're talkin' about.'

'That's a load of bullshit, Barnes,' snapped Wells. 'You'll never get to spend that money so you might as well show us where it is.'

'I know that,' said Ephram, laughing. 'That's 'cos I don't know where it is.'

Eventually the meat was cooked and shared out among the six of them and was greatly appreciated. Since it seemed obvious that Ephram was not about to reveal the whereabouts of the money, Barney Wells gave up trying. He did confide in Caleb in a brief moment when they were alone that unless they found the money there was no way he could detain Ephram.

'I don't suppose you could have got this all wrong?' he asked Caleb.

'I only know what I saw and heard,' said Caleb.

'The money is here somewhere, I am certain of that.'

'Yeah, I guess so,' admitted Barney. 'Only trouble is I can't afford much more time lookin' for it. If we haven't found it by about midday tomorrow, I'll have to leave an' let Barnes go. The important thing is to get Parker an' Smith back to Kernville. It would be nice to be able to take the money back as well. I know they're both wanted for other things an' I'll make sure you get your reward, but without the money it's goin' to be difficult to prove they robbed the bank.'

'Then let's hope we find it soon,' said Caleb.

'Maybe you'd better have words with your friend up there,' suggested Wells, looking skyward.

FIVE

The search was resumed at dawn the following morning and continued until just after midday, when Barney Wells eventually called a halt. In that time five more caves had been discovered but in each case there had been no sign that anything had been hidden or that the floor had recently been disturbed. During the morning, Caleb noticed a satisfied smile on Ephram's face, which seemed to become even more smug the further they progressed along the ridge. That smile told him that there was little prospect of the money being found in any other caves they might discover. However, he chose not to make his observations known to Deputy Marshal Barnaby Wells.

'As much as I would like to carry on,' said Barney, 'I just can't afford the time. I'll arrange for a search party to continue looking when I get back to Kernville.'

'I'll see to it,' volunteered Matt McCauly. 'I reckon it shouldn't be too difficult to find folk ready to look, especially with the prospect of a reward if they find it.'

'It'd sure save a lot of time,' agreed Barney. 'OK, Matt, I'll leave it to you.'

'Does that mean I won't get the reward if it is found?' asked Caleb.

'That's somethin' you'll have to sort out with the bank and the lawyers,' said Wells. 'I ain't no lawyer, I don't know who'd have the right to any reward money.'

'Maybe we can come to some arrangement,' said Matt. 'If I arrange a search party an' they do find it, it seems only fair that they should get at least half.'

'I suppose so,' conceded Caleb. 'OK, I'll agree to that.'

'What about me?' asked Ephram. 'You can't hold me, you can't prove nothin', so I reckon I'm free to go.'

'Unfortunately, you are right,' said Barney, sighing heavily. 'OK, Barnes, you can go, but don't bank on stayin' free. If I get so much as one whisper that you know where the money is, I'll have you locked up quicker'n a jack rabbit can run. Do you understand just what I'm sayin' – *Mister* Barnes?'

'I hear you loud an' clear, Marshal,' sneered Ephram. 'Did I ever tell you I can outrun any jack rabbit?'

They made their way back along the ridge and when they reached the point where the ridge came closest to Ephram's trading post, he grunted something which nobody understood and rode off. Caleb continued on with Wells and McCauly for about ten minutes before he too stopped and looked back.

'I'll be in Kernville as soon as I can, so don't go giving that reward for Parker and Smith to anyone else,' he told Barney Wells. 'I'm going to follow

Ephram. There was something about the way he was acting that makes me think somebody ought to follow him.'

'Good idea,' agreed Wells. 'I still think he knows where the money is. You just be careful, Reverend, I wouldn't trust that man not to kill you if you get in his way. That amount of money could test a saint.'

'I might be a preacher but I am certainly no saint,' said Caleb. 'Don't worry though, if I do get my hands on it, I will be satisfied with the reward. I can look after myself when I have to. Years of drifting and four years in the army have taught me a thing or two. If I do turn up dead, at least you'll know who did it.'

'You were in the army?' asked Wells. 'On which side? I hear that even the Confederates had some black troops.'

'I was a lieutenant in command of an all-black infantry company on the Union side,' said Caleb. 'This is one black preacher who learned to be a preacher the hard way. I'll be seeing you, gentlemen.' He touched the brim of his hat, laughed at them and then made his way back in the general direction of the trading post.

He had been travelling about an hour when, on cresting a hill, he saw Ephram riding furiously back in the direction of Bailey's Ridge. It was obvious that Ephram had not seen him and, after allowing him a few minutes to get ahead, Caleb followed.

When they reached the ridge, he was not at all surprised when Ephram leapt from his horse and ran towards some bushes half-way up the slope. Keeping well out of sight, he waited for Ephram to reappear, which he did rather more quickly than

Caleb expected. The look on Ephram's face as he clambered on to his horse, empty handed and cursing loudly, told Caleb all that he needed to know. The money had been there but was not there now. Ephram raced off, this time in the direction of Broken Ridge but Caleb did not follow. Instead, out of little more than idle curiosity, he decided to look inside what he presumed to be a cave.

The entrance was low and narrow, but just large enough for a man to squeeze himself through. It was little more than a hole, about eight feet across and four or five feet high. There was nothing to be seen, although Caleb did a fingertip search in the semi-darkness just to be certain. He was quite convinced that this was where the money had been stored but that it was no longer there, which plainly meant that someone else had been there before Ephram. He smiled knowingly and headed back towards the trading post.

The scene which greeted Caleb was rather unexpected; all that remained of the building were a few, fire-blackened uprights and what had been the contents of the trading post, a few piles still smouldering.

He made a brief search among the charred remains but there was no sign of Esther either dead or alive and Caleb was not at all surprised. If she or her body had been there it would have thrown his theory into disarray. Now, however, he was quite certain as to what had happened.

'She Who Makes Trouble! That's what she said her Indian name meant. I now see just why,' Caleb said to himself. 'This time, She Who Makes Trouble, I think you have created rather more trouble for yourself than you can handle on your own.'

To be doubly sure that nothing had happened to Esther, he made a cursory search of the nearby woods before making his way back to Broken Ridge, but again found no evidence that she had been murdered.

'Well, neither of them have been through here,' asserted Matt McCauly. 'I'd've heard about it if they had. Are you quite certain her body ain't out there somewheres. It'd give us a reason to arrest Ephram.'

'Well I for one am pleased that you can't arrest him for that reason,' said Caleb. 'I think though, that should Ephram catch up with her, you will certainly have your reason. It is obvious to me that she knew far more than she admitted to, even to the extent of knowing exactly where the money had been hidden.'

'I'll go along with that,' agreed Matt. 'OK, so she now has upwards of thirty-seven thousand dollars. That's a lot of money an' I can't see her not lettin' it go to her head, she just ain't used to it. She's probably never seen more'n ten dollars in one place in her life before. Now where do you think a woman with that much money would head for?'

'Well she'd steer well clear of Broken Ridge and Kernville, that's for sure. She's not that stupid,' said Caleb. 'What is the nearest town beyond Kernville?'

'Don't rightly know,' replied Matt. 'Probably Whithorn, about two hundred miles due north. You can't rely on that though. These days it seems that new towns are bein' built all over the place, especially when there's gold about.'

'Does this Whithorn have a railroad station?' asked Caleb.

'Railroad!' said Matt. 'No, I don't think so. The nearest place for a railroad is Kernville.'

'Then I believe it is most unlikely that she would try to get to Whithorn,' said Caleb. 'I had a talk with her, when she told me about the robbery being planned. She told me then that she wanted to go to San Francisco. I think that is where she is headed right now.'

'Then she sure as hell wouldn't come this way,' said Matt. 'The shortest way is through River Bend, but they don't have the railroad there either. San Francisco's in California ain't it?' Caleb nodded. 'That's one hell of a long way.'

'Long way or not, I believe that is where she intends to go,' said Caleb.

'Well, if she has, I reckon you can say goodbye to ever gettin' that money back.' said Matt. 'Even if she gets caught, chances are there won't be much of it left an' I know enough about the law to know that it'd be almost impossible to prove that she stole the money. No, sir, she's the wrong side of the State line, even federal marshals can't touch her down there, not without special warrants and agreements an' they're damned hard to come by.'

'I suppose you are right,' conceded Caleb. 'Anyway, at least I know I've got two thousand dollars coming; I suppose I shall have to be satisfied with that.'

'Any man ought to be satisfied with that much,' grunted Matt. 'I sure wish it was comin' to me. This job could go to hell if it was. I got my eye on a small farm up near the Snake River. Good land an' good fishin'.'

'I hope you get it,' sighed Caleb. 'OK, I suppose it's hardly worth the bother of going after her. She will just have to take her chance with Ephram. I've just about outstayed my welcome in Broken Ridge, so I might as well move on. I'll go to Kernville first and collect my money. After that it's anyone's guess as to where I'll end up. I had thought about heading up towards Seattle. I knew a man from there once who was always saying what a wonderful place it was.'

'I heard of it, that's about all I can say,' said Matt. 'I don't know about Mrs Higgins an' the others, but I for one will be kind of sorry to see you go. At least you brought some life into this dreary town for a change.'

'I don't suppose Maud Higgins will be all that sorry,' said Caleb. 'There's a new minister due at the end of next month, or so she told me.'

'Yeah, a young feller from what I heard,' said Matt. 'Frances Day sure won't like that.'

In actual fact, Caleb decided that the best thing he could do would be to simply ride out of Broken Ridge without a word of farewell to anyone, even Frances Day. Accordingly, just before dawn the following morning, he quietly, and largely unseen, left the town.

Deputy US Marshal Barnaby Wells listened to Caleb's story and theory as to what had happened and was forced to concede that it was the most likely scenario. He also agreed with Matt McCauly that the chances of recovering the money were indeed rather remote. It had now been four days at least since Esther had made off with it, which gave her a big advantage.

'As far as I know, Ephram Barnes hasn't been through here,' he told Caleb. 'You said he rode off in the direction of Broken Ridge. I figure that's because his place had burned down an' he needed supplies if nothin' else. I know he was friendly with a couple of farmers not far from his place. It's my bet he went to one of them for help of some kind. After that I'd say he too went on through River Bend. I don't fancy that young lady's chances at all.'

'I wouldn't write her off quite so easily,' said Caleb. 'I have the feeling that she is quite capable of looking after herself if she needs to. She must have learned a few things about survival from the Indians.'

'An' she's goin' to need all she knows to survive down there an' get to San Francisco,' said Wells. 'OK, Reverend, let's go and sort out this reward. Two thousand is a hell of a lot of money, just what are you goin' to do with it?'

Caleb laughed. 'I've had more than that before,' he said. 'Every time I say I'm going to save it or settle down somewhere, but somehow that never seems to happen. Do you have a map? I'd like to look at it to help me make up my mind.'

'Sure, there's one here somewhere,' replied Wells. He eventually found a large map and left Caleb to look over it while he went along to the bank to make arrangements for the payment of the reward.

Without really thinking about it, Caleb found himself tracing the line of the railroad as it meandered westward. Where it passed through a town called Hazel, he saw that another railroad also joined the town, this time coming from the south-east. Once again he drew his finger along the route and grunted. He double-checked the route and a smile slowly spread across his face. This railroad passed through a town called Tarriopah which appeared to be fairly close to River Bend.

'Now if she's heading for San Francisco,' he mused, 'I think she'll make her way to this Tarriopah place and then to Hazel.' He picked up the town of Hazel again and noted that from there both rail-roads merged, headed southwest and eventually ended up in southern California at Los Angeles.

Between Hazel and the final destination of the railroad, there were several stops. The nearest to San Francisco seemed to be a small town called Lone Pine, not far inside the California border.

'I wonder!' he said to himself. 'Yes, I think so. She'll want to get to San Francisco as quickly as she can and by the easiest route. Caleb, it's been a long time since you were in California and since you don't have anything better to do. . . . Yes, why not?'

Two hours later the reward money had been paid and Caleb wandered down to the railroad station. He was in luck, there was a westbound train due to leave in less than an hour. He booked himself a first class seat as far as Hazel, booked his horse into a freight wagon and an hour later saw the town of Kernville disappear.

The journey to Hazel was slow and took just over twenty-four hours, twenty four hours during which the other occupants of the first class carriage at first looked at him with suspicion, obviously amazed that a negro could afford to travel first class. He over-heard conversations questioning why the railroad company had allowed a negro to travel that way, even if he was a preacher. He simply acknowledged their scowls with a polite nod of his head.

Hazel proved to be a town slightly larger than Kernville, apparently built around two lumber mills. The main difference was that it also housed an army cavalry regiment. Finding accommodation in the town proved very difficult. Rooming-houses which carried vacancy signs were suddenly full when Caleb presented himself. This did not really bother him, he was used to such things and he had just about resigned himself to moving out of town and sleeping rough for the night when, at the last rooming-house he tried, he discovered that the owner was also a black woman.

'Well, mercy me!' beamed the enormous Mrs Sylvester. 'It ain't often we gets preachers. I take it you is a preacher, you sure looks like one.' Caleb assured her that he was. 'Well now, come on in, Reverend, come on in. How long are you stayin'?'

'Just the one night,' said Caleb. 'I'm on the first train out in the morning.'

'I should have guessed,' she said, laughing. 'Ain't nobody stays in Hazel more'n one night, 'specially black folk. Now it wouldn't be right for a preacher to share a room, so I'll give you the front room. It ain't too big but at least you won't have no sweaty bodies an' snorin' to keep you awake. I see you got a horse. Most folk don't have horses, especially black fellers. There's a livery stable just along the street. Are you takin' the horse down south with you?'

'Thank you, Mrs Sylvester,' said Caleb. 'It's much

appreciated. Yes, the horse goes with me. We've been together a long time and I just couldn't be parted from her. Do you have many other guests?'

'I got three other black fellers,' she said. 'They live here more or less permanently. There's a few others in the town, but no more'n half a dozen. I reckon you is probably hungry. I'll cook you somethin' special.' Once again Caleb thanked her and found himself being ushered into a small but clean room containing a narrow bed, a small table and a rickety looking chair. 'You just settle yourself in an' don't you worry none about the horse, my boy will see to it. Just one thing, I'd take off the saddle an' anythin' else, things have a habit of goin' missin' round here. I'll call you when supper's ready.' Caleb went downstairs and removed the saddle which, at her insistence, he left in Mrs Sylvester's private room.

Back in his room, Caleb stood gazing out of the window for a while, wondering if he was doing the sensible thing. His concern was no longer for the money but he still felt concern for Esther. Suddenly, he pulled back out of sight and peered out of the window. There was no mistake; walking along on the opposite side of the street was Ephram Barnes.

'It looks like I was right,' he said to himself. 'The next question is, is she in town as well? I think that after supper I'll have a look around.' He saw Ephram enter a rather seedy-looking rooming-house further along the street. 'At least I know where you are, Mr Barnes.'

Mrs Sylvester's son knocked timidly on the door and announced that supper was ready. Caleb followed the boy downstairs and was shown into a

small room furnished with a single rough wooden
table and two benches. There were three other men
seated, waiting for supper and all three stood up
when he entered, one of the men snatching a
battered hat off the head of the man next to him.

'Good evening, gentlemen,' said Caleb, looking
with some dismay at the large bowl of unappetizing
stew which was being placed on the table by Mrs
Sylvester. The men mumbled in reply and looked
uneasily at both Caleb and Mrs Sylvester.

'Mercy me, Reverend,' said Mrs Sylvester. 'You
ain't eatin' in here. I told that useless son of mine to
show you into my room. He don't ever listen to what
I say.'

'Most boys don't,' said Caleb. 'Please, gentlemen,
carry on with your meal.' He followed Mrs Sylvester
through to her private room.

'I seen the way you looked at that mess of stew,
Reverend,' she said, almost apologetically. 'Don't
you worry none 'bout that, I got somethin' special
for you. Here sit yourself down.' She pulled out a
chair by the table. 'I'll bet you ain't tasted nothin'
like what I got since you was a kid. You ain't married
are you?' Caleb shook his head and smiled. 'Didn't
think you was, you don't look married.'

'And how does a married man look?' asked Caleb.

'Oh, you know,' she said. 'It's hard to describe. A
married man just sort of looks ... well ... sort of
looks married.' She burst out laughing. 'Now you
just sit down.' She went through a door and
returned carrying a large serving dish which she
placed on the table with a theatrical flourish.
'There!' she said, proudly. 'I'll bet you ain't had goat
for a good while. That's fresh goat meat, baked plan-

tains, yams, an' pumpkin. I'll bet you ain't had anythin' like this in many a year.'

'Indeed I haven't,' said Caleb, almost afraid to tell her that pumpkin was his least favourite vegetable. 'Really, Mrs Sylvester, you shouldn't have gone to all this trouble.'

'Trouble!' she said, laughing. 'It ain't no trouble at all. We eats like this all the time.'

'Is there a Mr Sylvester?' asked Caleb.

'Sure is,' she replied with a large smile. 'There's been a Mr Sylvester for the past twenty-five years. This is my youngest son, he's just ten years old. I got two other children, a boy an' a girl, they is both twenty-somethin'. James here came as somethin' of a surprise.' She laughed rather coarsely. Caleb was actually quite relieved to hear that there was a Mr Sylvester. 'My man an' the eldest boy work down at the Pearson lumber mill. They ain't due home for another couple of hours. My daughter's got a good job at the Majestic Hotel.' She laughed again. 'They don't mind blacks workin' there but they won't have 'em stayin' as guests. No blacks an' no Indians, that's the rule. She's due home any time now.'

'I know, I tried there,' said Caleb.

At that moment a young, shapely woman came into the room and looked rather startled when she saw Caleb. Her mother introduced the preacher.

'I was just tellin' the Reverend that they don't take black folk down at the Majestic,' she said. 'He says he already tried there.'

'Yes,' nodded the daughter, Naomi, 'I saw him. I would have thought that a place like the Majestic was out of the reach of even a black preacher.'

'I am in the fortunate position of being able to

pay my way,' replied Caleb.

'Just shows you can't always judge,' said Naomi. She looked at Caleb rather curiously. 'The Reverend Caleb Black,' she said. 'Now it'd be too much of a coincidence if there were two Reverend Caleb Blacks. Weren't you in Broken Ridge not all that long ago?'

Caleb looked at her sharply. 'Indeed I was,' he confirmed. 'How did you know that? I only arrived on the train from Kernville this afternoon and as far as I know I do not know anyone in Hazel.'

Naomi looked rather self-conscious. 'Maybe I've said too much,' she said.

'Please,' insisted Caleb. 'I am intrigued. How could you possibly know?' Naomi glanced at her mother and licked her lips. Mrs Sylvester nodded and Naomi looked at Caleb.

'Well, I guess it can't do no harm, she ain't here now,' said Naomi. 'We had a young woman stayin' at the hotel for a couple of days. There was somethin' about the way she dressed which didn't look right. Mr Jacobs – he's the manager – wasn't even sure if he ought to allow her to stay. He reckoned she looked too much like an Indian an' Indians ain't allowed. Anyhow, it seems that she wasn't really an Indian but had been raised by Indians. Mr Jacobs still wasn't too sure but she seemed to have plenty of money so he gave in.'

'She Who Makes Trouble!' said Caleb.'

'She Who . . . Yeah, that's it,' said Naomi. 'That's what she said her Indian name meant. Anyhow, me an' her got to talkin' – I'm a chambermaid at the hotel – an' she told me to keep my eye open for somebody named Ephram, Ephram Barnes I think

she said.' She laughed. 'Hell, it ain't much use tryin'
to tell someone like me what a white feller looks like
unless he's got three legs or two heads, they all look
the same to me. Anyhow, I said I'd keep a watch out
– didn't see nobody though.'

'He's in a rooming-house just up the street,' said
Caleb. Naomi looked surprised.

'Yeah, well maybe he is,' she said. 'Anyhow, like I
said, we got to talkin' an' she told me about you. At
least she told me about a black preacher by the
name of Caleb Black an' I presume that's you. She
said you were the only man, black or white, ever to
show her any kindness. She told me about this
Ephram feller, too.'

'Ephram is half black,' said Caleb. 'Didn't she tell
you that?'

'No, she never mentioned it,' said Naomi. 'Maybe
if she had I might've recognized him. Anyhow, she
told me about how he used to beat her an' how she
finally had too much an' walked out on him.'

'I suppose you could say she did that,' said Caleb.
'Where is she now? Believe me, I need to know. It is
most important that I reach her before Ephram
Barnes does. If he gets to her first she's a dead
woman. Believe me, I do not intend her any harm. I
just want to help her.'

'Sure, I know that, Reverend,' said Naomi. 'Right
now I'd say she was on her way to San Francisco.'

'She was here two days ago!' said Caleb. 'How can
she be on her way to San Francisco? I was told there
are only two trains a week, one on Monday morning
and one tomorrow morning. She couldn't have
caught the Monday train.'

'She wasn't prepared to stay any longer'n she

could,' replied Naomi. 'She said somethin' about buyin' a horse.'

'And did she?'

'I don't rightly know,' said Naomi. 'All I know is she left town.'

SIX

Caleb, along with everyone else in the Sylvester household, was up at dawn. Mrs Sylvester insisted that he ate a good breakfast before he left and would not take no for an answer. When he had eaten, Caleb went along to the livery stable and, whilst he was saddling his horse, asked about Esther. He was in luck, a young woman answering her description had indeed purchased a horse and saddle.

'I warned her that it wasn't safe for a woman to be out ridin' alone,' said the livery owner. 'Especially when she said somethin' about headin' west to San Francisco. That's wild country up there an' at this time of year it gets mighty cold. Then there's robbers an' Indians to contend with. She said she wasn't bothered about no Indians an' that any robbers would soon find out she could look after herself. I told her the best thing she could do was wait for the train this mornin'. She was havin' none of it though.'

'I can understand why she wasn't bothered about Indians,' said Caleb. 'She was raised by them and I can well believe that she would give a good account

84

of herself with any robbers. You don't happen to know exactly which way she went do you?'

'All I told her was that there wasn't any easy way,' he replied. 'I'm pretty sure she started out headin' for Smoke Creek Desert an' Honey Lake. That's due west.'

'Thanks,' muttered Caleb. 'Oh, just one more thing . . .' he tantalizingly fingered a ten dollar bill, 'there just might be someone else asking about her, a half-blood negro by the name of Ephram Barnes. This ten dollars says that you have not seen or heard of either her or me.'

'I ain't never seen either of you in my life,' he grunted, snatching the money.

Before leaving Hazel, Caleb bought a few supplies from the nearest general store. Although he kept a constant look out, he did not see Ephram and as far as he knew, Ephram had not seen him. A short time later Caleb was riding out of town towards Smoke Creek Desert, a route which, he had been assured, very few people chose.

Crossing deserts was not a new experience to Caleb and, although Smoke Creek Desert looked much like any other, it differed in that the strong wind which blew from the west was very cold indeed. In the far distance, the Sierra Nevada mountains appeared to be covered in snow and the one thing he really disliked was snow. At that point he started to wonder whether or not following Esther was a big mistake. However, having come this far and being basically a bloody-minded person, he kept going.

Crossing the desert took two days, during which time he saw no other sign of life apart from one lizard, two rattlesnakes and a solitary buzzard look-ing for a meal. Neither was there any sign of water and his meagre water supply had all but been exhausted – mostly given to his horse. Gradually, however, the grass seemed to become a little greener and the occasional thorn-tree appeared. By mid-afternoon of the third day he came across a fairly large pool of clear water set amongst some rocks. It was here that he discovered his first real evidence that Esther or someone was ahead of him.

There had been a fire and the embers, although cold, seemed comparatively fresh. There was plenty of old timber lying about so he too lit a fire and resolved to rest there the remainder of the day. He needed the rest but, more importantly, so did his horse. There was plenty of grazing for his horse but the only food he had was some dried beef and a portion of cheese. He chose to eat the cheese. That night proved very cold and Caleb spent most of it making sure the fire was kept burning. He supposed that he must have slept some of the time, particu-larly in the period just before dawn.

At about midday he came across a large lake which he assumed to be the Honey Lake he had been told about. A solitary, run-down cabin on the lake side showed that someone else had recently taken shelter there. It seemed a little too soon for Esther to have rested up again – if the embers of the previous fire had been hers and he came to the conclusion that someone else was also heading in the same direction.

At first he wondered if it might be Ephram Barnes, but he considered this unlikely since he had seen Ephram in Hazel and, unless he had started out that same night, it was impossible for him to have reached that far. The discovery of a cheroot butt told him that whoever it was who had stayed in this cabin, it was not Esther.

'I suppose it is possible that there could be others making their way westward,' he said to himself. 'It just seems rather too much of a coincidence though. Yes, She Who Makes Trouble, I think you have made rather more trouble for yourself than you intended.'

It was about midday the following day that Caleb came across the second cabin situated in a small hollow alongside what appeared to be long abandoned mine workings. This time, however, there were three horses hobbled nearby. He looked for a way past but there was no other route. He had to go almost right up to the cabin.

The cabin itself gave the impression of being in an advanced state of decay. Although the roof and walls seemed intact, the door hung loosely and the only two windows he could see obviously had no frames. The remains of an ancient window drape fluttered in the wind.

Caleb had little desire to confront anyone he did not have to. It was quite possible that the three men he assumed to be inside were bandits and robbers and he knew for certain that such men would take great delight in making life very difficult for him, despite his clerical garb or even because of it, and all the more so because of his colour. He remained behind some large rocks, upon the top of which he lay flat and watched.

He had been there about half an hour when a large, very hairy man appeared, slamming the rickety door, an act which persuaded the door to finally part company with the only hinge. The man simply laughed coarsely and proceeded to obey the call of nature outside the door. Another man, this time obviously the worse for drink judging by the fact that he was very unsteady on his feet and was waving a bottle about, joined him. The man took a long drink and passed the bottle to the first man who apparently drained it since he threw it to one side in obvious disgust. The first man returned inside the cabin and almost immediately there was a loud, coarse laugh, followed by a woman rushing from the cabin. She was held by the second man and forced to the ground. Caleb, however, had already grabbed his rifle. He had seen enough to know that the woman was Esther.

The distance between Caleb and the cabin was about a hundred yards and as such was at the extreme limit of the range of his rifle to ensure an accurate shot. There was certainly no question of attempting to shoot the man now wrestling with Esther since he was just as likely to hit her. The other man emerged from the cabin and joined the man on the ground with Esther. Caleb decided that it was now time to make his move.

Slowly and quietly Caleb made his way towards them until he was within ten yards. They seemed completely oblivious to his approach. He paused for a moment before speaking.

'I think the lady does not like your attentions, gentlemen,' he said. 'I suggest that you get up, very slowly, and do not attempt to use your guns.'

Both men looked up and stared at the stranger unbelievingly but neither of them moved. Eventually the bearded man spoke.

'An' just who the hell are you?' he slurred. 'Hell, Silas, we got us a negro. Silas gave a drunken leer, revealing a mouthful of blackened teeth. 'Well now, since when did the likes of you care about what happens to a white woman?'

'As of this moment,' said Caleb, 'this rifle tells me I care a lot. Get up before I forget that I am a minister of the Lord and kill you where you are. I can assure you that even I cannot miss from this range.'

'Minister of . . .' spluttered Silas. 'Hell, Frank, we got us a preacher, a black preacher at that.' This time Esther twisted her head to look at Caleb and he was uncertain whether she was pleased to see him or not. The look on her face was certainly more of alarm than relief. 'Are you sure you know how to use that thing, *Reveren*?' Silas sneered. Caleb answered the question by firing a single shot which removed part of Silas's left ear. Silas seemed too astonished to cry out in pain, simply wiping his hand across the ear, glancing at the blood and then leering at Caleb. 'Yes, sir, I guess you do. OK, we're gettin' up. Come on Frank, do as the man says.'

Both men staggered to their feet and once again leered at Caleb. Frank also leered down at Esther who was attempting to cover her exposed body with her torn clothing.

'I reckon even a preacher likes a woman now an' then,' he rasped. 'Go ahead, Mr Preacherman, she's all yours. We've just about had our fill of her anyhow.'

'Are you badly hurt, Esther?' Caleb asked, ignoring the two men. Esther struggled to her feet and shook her head.

'You know this woman?' asked Silas. 'Yeah, I

reckon you do. If you know her then I reckon you also know what she's carryin'. Now you can have the woman, *Reveren'*, but there's no way you is goin' to take that money away from us.'

'That money was stolen from a bank in Kernville, all thirty-eight thousand of it,' said Caleb. 'I intend to return it to its rightful owners. I would imagine there is also a reward for you two as well. I might as well collect that as well.'

'Thirty-eight thou. . . !' exclaimed Frank. 'See, Silas, I *told* you there was more'n two thousand. I'll have to learn to count proper one of these days. So, you is a bounty hunter,' he continued. 'Since when did preachers take up bounty huntin'?'

'A man has to make a living,' said Caleb. 'Now, move away from her and drop your guns. I don't know how much you are worth dead, I'll just have to take that chance if necessary.'

'Preachers save men's souls, they ain't supposed to kill 'em,' said Silas.

'We all have our methods,' said Caleb with a broad grin. 'It's up to you, gentlemen, dead or alive, I don't much care which.'

The two men stepped away from Esther and dropped their gunbelts as instructed. Caleb lowered the rifle and instructed Esther to pick up their guns. He indicated that they should make their way back to the cabin. As they turned, they both casually slipped their hands beneath their jackets. Casually, but not quite casually enough.

Caleb was forced to admit that both men were very fast and reasonably accurate. Had they been sober they would probably have been even more accurate and the result might well have been very different. One bullet scraped the side of his temple and the other ripped through his coat sleeve. Caleb's two bullets on the other hand, one from each of his Colt pistols, thudded with deadly accuracy into each man's chest. An examination was simply not necessary as far as Caleb was concerned. There was little doubt in his mind that both were dead.

He smiled at Esther. 'At least they'll be a lot less trouble dead,' he said. 'I believe you told the man at the livery stable in Hazel that you could look after yourself. I suppose if you call this looking after yourself then you have. What happened?'

'What happened to me doesn't matter,' she responded. 'What the hell are you doin' out here? I thought you might've taken up the job of minister in Broken Ridge. I know that Mrs Day sure had the hots for you.'

'I would have thought the reason I am here would be obvious,' said Caleb. 'I came looking for you. It would seem that I am not the only one either.' He looked down at the bodies. 'I have the feeling that these two didn't come across you by accident. Ephram was in Hazel as well. I suspect it will not be all that long before he finds out which way you went. He might even have found out by now and be on his way.'

'Ephram I was expectin',' she said. 'You I was not. OK, Mr Black, what happens now?'

'I take the money back to Kernville,' said Caleb. 'You can come along if you like, I don't think anyone will bother pressing any charges against you.'

'And Ephram?' she asked.

'I'll deal with him if and when necessary,' replied

Caleb. 'These two might be worth a few dollars, we can drop them off in Hazel.'

'They followed me from Hazel,' said Esther. 'I remember them hanging around. I think they guessed I had plenty of money and thought I would be easy pickings.'

'And it would seem that they were right,' said Caleb with a knowing smile. 'It was perhaps as well I happened along, I rather fancy they were about to kill you. They'd probably finished with you. I must admit that I had not expected to come across you so soon, although the signs were that they were following you. I would have thought that your years with the Indians might have taught you something about the art of survival.'

'My horse went lame,' she said. 'I was resting up when they appeared. One minute I was on my own an' the next minute they were burstin' in. They kept me here for two days,' she spat at the bodies. 'I lost count of the number of times they raped me. I suppose I have to thank you for the fact that I'm still alive.'

'I expect no thanks,' said Caleb. 'How much of the money is left?'

'Most of it,' said Esther. 'I spent maybe two hundred or just over at the most.'

'I dare say the bank will be very satisfied,' he said. 'Now, I suggest that we remain here until tomorrow morning. Is there anything to eat in the cabin?'

'One of them had shot a deer,' she said. 'There's still some of it left.'

'Then it will have to do,' said Caleb. 'I'm hungry, you can prepare some food while I get my horse.' Something told Caleb that, for his own safety, he needed to check the cabin. She scowled at him but remained silent as she obediently returned to the cabin, closely followed by Caleb. Inside the cabin he found a rifle which he held up questioningly. She simply nodded, confirming that it did belong to her. He checked for other weapons and found none but again, to be safe, he took her rifle and the guns belonging to the dead men with him when he went to recover his horse.

Back inside the cabin, it was obvious that Silas and Frank had been throwing the money about and it took Caleb quite some time to gather it together. He counted it back into the carpet-bag in which Esther had been carrying it.

'Well?' she asked. 'How much is there?'

'Thirty-seven thousand seven hundred and sixty dollars,' he said 'Allowing for you having spent about two hundred and forty, that makes a total of thirty-eight thousand.'

'And they were arguing about whether or not it was more than two thousand,' she laughed. 'I can't count that good either, but I knew it was a hell of a lot more'n that.' She looked at Caleb and thrust out her bosom. 'Almost thirty-eight thousand. I never knew there was that much money in the world. That's a hell of a lot of money, Reverend, more'n enough for the both of us.' She moved closer to him. 'Half the money an' me! I reckon that's a fair deal.'

Caleb laughed and gently pushed her to one side. 'I am a minister of the church, remember,' he said. 'I do not steal from anyone.'

'Hell!' she snapped. 'It ain't the same as stealin'! I mean, it ain't as if you actually stole it off anyone. I didn't actually steal it from the bank either. In fact I don't even know if it really does belong to the damned bank. In any case, they can afford it. As far as I'm concerned I found it an' findin' is nine tenths of the law from what I've been told.'

'Then you have been misinformed,' said Caleb. 'You make it sound so very easy, Esther, but as far as I'm concerned it still belongs to the bank. I shall be satisfied with the ten per cent reward.'

She stormed back to the fire and furiously turned the meat.

'Just how the hell did you know where I was?' she eventually demanded. 'I didn't even know where I was headed myself. I ended up out here by accident.'

'My dear young lady,' said Caleb, sarcastically. 'I have long since come to the conclusion that you are quite incapable of doing anything by accident. You knew exactly where the money was hidden and you deliberately planned to take it. As for my knowing where you were, I must admit that was more of a gamble on my part. Do you remember telling me that it was your ambition to get to San Francisco?' She nodded weakly. 'Well, all I had to do was look at a map and work out which way you would go. I suspect that you did something very similar.'

'Me an' my big mouth,' she grumbled. 'If I'd known you was a bounty hunter when I went to church, I wouldn't have gone anywhere near you. OK, so I planned it all down to the last detail did I? Well I've got news for you, Reverend, I didn't plan a damned thing. Sure, I guessed where Ephram had hidden that money. We'd both been up there before, huntin' deer, an' we came across that small cave by accident. Ephram said at the time that it would be a good place to hide things. When they decided to rob the bank and hide the money, I just figured that Ephram would choose that place.' She laughed. 'He ain't none too bright when it comes to workin' things out.'

'Bright enough to have worked out which way you went,' said Caleb.

'Yeah, well, maybe so,' she conceded. 'Anyhow, when you took him and the other two into Broken Ridge I figured that was the last I was goin' to see of him. I went lookin' for the money and it was where I thought it would be. After that I set out for River Bend. I guess you know the rest.'

'Why did you set fire to the trading post?' asked Caleb.

'It just seemed a good idea at the time,' she said, laughing. 'I never thought Ephram would be freed. Anyhow, it wouldn't've mattered, he'd've soon found out the money was missing and with me gone even he would have been able to work out what had happened. I must admit I got a terrific thrill at seeing it goin' up in flames. It was just like a bad dream comin' to an end.'

'I don't think Ephram was very pleased,' said Caleb. 'So then you made your way to Tarriopah and caught the train as far as Hazel. I had it worked out that you would leave the train at a place called Lone Pine and from there make your way across country to San Francisco.'

'I thought about that,' she admitted. 'My original idea though, was to take the train to Los Angeles an' from there work my way up the coast to San Francisco. I heard once that there are regular boats from Los Angeles to San Francisco. I ain't never seen the sea. They tell me it's nothin' but water for as far as the eye can see. Water you can't even drink on account of it bein' salty. Fish live in it though, I don't understand that. Anyhow, I sort of fancied takin' a ferry on it. The only ferry I've ever been on was the one across the Snake River up the other side of Broken Ridge. All that was was a flat-bottomed punt about ten feet long. I hear you could fit a whole town into some of the boats on the sea.'

'Some of them are very big,' said Caleb. 'I've only ever seen them once and that was a good many years ago. So what made you change your mind?'

'There was a feller in Hazel I knew quite well who came from River Bend,' she said. 'I don't think he saw me but he seemed to know about the robbery in Kernville and how he thought Ephram was tied up in it. I overheard him talkin' about it. I figured that if he saw me he might tell the sheriff. I just sort of panicked I suppose an' decided to get the hell out of it there an' then.'

'And these two followed you,' he said. 'Then I followed you and I strongly suspect that Ephram is now also on his way. I don't think you could have done a better job of it if you had advertised your intentions in the newspaper at Hazel.'

'Yeah, I suppose I did mess things up.' She sighed. 'I seem to remember, Reverend, you making some sort of promise to give me two thousand dollars when you recovered this money. Well now, I figure that now you've got your hands on it, you ought to honour your promise.'

'I didn't agree on two thousand,' said Caleb. 'That was your idea. It is true, I did make some sort of rash suggestion that I might help you out. That was before you tried running off with the money though. As things stand I think you ought to thank the Lord that you are still alive.'

'Just as I figured,' she sighed. 'Even a preacher can't be trusted to keep his word. Don't you worry about me though, I'll survive.'

'I have little doubt that you will,' he conceded.

The night turned very cold again and they both gathered as much wood as they could, intent on keeping warm that night. The four horses were also led into the cabin and tethered at the far end. There was not a lot of room but at least they were warm.

How long it was after they turned in for the night, Caleb had no idea. All he remembered was being woken up by a strange sound. He looked into the gloom just in time to see Esther standing about five feet away with a rifle aimed at him. He also vaguely remembered hearing the shot, but that was all. . . .

SEVEN

A severe pain had the effect of making Caleb feel as though someone was battering him about the head with an iron bar. At first he had great difficulty in focusing his eyes but eventually he realized that his lack of vision was due, in the main, to blood having congealed over his face. After clearing his eyes he gingerly felt his head and winced when his fingers discovered a wound about an inch above his left eye. His touch told him that it was little more than a graze, but it certainly appeared to have bled rather more than he might have expected judging by the amount of blood on his head and jacket. By that time he had also realized that it was daylight and he groggily staggered to his feet and went outside.

There was a water butt alongside one of the old mine-workings and, tightly gripping the rim, he plunged his head into the icy water. As well as washing the blood off his face, the coldness also served to revive him. After satisfying himself that the wound was indeed superficial, he returned to the cabin and was somewhat surprised to find that his and the dead men's horses were still there. That had been something he had not noticed before. However, there was no need to search for the money, it was obvious that it had disappeared along with Esther.

'Very well, She Who Makes Trouble,' he muttered. 'If you want to play rough, I suppose I shall have to show you just how rough even a preacher can be. I've come too far to give in now.'

Before leaving, Caleb fixed hobbles round the front feet of the other two horses and then turned them loose. He then wrapped the bodies of the two men in their blankets and carried them into the cabin. Next, he boarded up the door and the windows, his prime motive being to prevent foxes, buzzards and other scavengers from getting at the bodies. He did realize that a determined fox would soon find a way inside but there was little else he could do. It was his intention to retrieve the bodies and the horses later.

Following Esther's trail proved very easy, even to a man of Caleb's limited tracking ability. He had to assume that she thought he was dead and there was no need to hide signs of her progress. According to his watch, it had been almost midday when he had eventually started out. What time it had been when Esther had shot him he had no idea, just as he had no idea as to what time she had left the cabin. Whatever time that had been, by sunset he did not appear to have made any headway on her.

It was mid-morning the following day when he came across a faded sign pointing along a narrow, steep-sided valley, indicating that somewhere called Emerson was ten miles ahead. There was another trail which climbed steeply up the side of the valley but logic told him that Esther would choose the easier route. He did wonder for a few moments if logic also told Esther which way to go. A few yards along the trail the indications were that he was right. There were new scuff-marks on some rocks set across the trail. Apart from Esther's recent journey, the track gave the very definite impression that it had not been used for a long time.

The town of Emerson – at least that was what the sign proclaimed it to be – consisted of a solitary store, four shacks which appeared to be lived in and the remains of what had, at some time in the past, apparently been quite a sizeable community. The vast majority of the buildings were now little more than piles of rotting wood. His arrival was witnessed by two men lounging about on what remained of a boardwalk outside the store, an elderly woman pounding some washing on a flat stone in a nearby stream and a solitary Indian wearing an old US cavalry hat and jacket. The Indian disappeared shortly after Caleb tethered his horse outside the store where he quite deliberately removed his rifle from the saddle holster, not prepared to trust anyone not to attempt to steal it even in such a small community.

'Good morning, gentlemen,' greeted Caleb as he mounted the protesting timbers of the boardwalk. 'Do I have the honour of addressing the owner of this establishment?' Both men looked at him blankly for a few moments as though he spoke in some foreign language. One of them slowly took a long draw at an apparently lifeless clay pipe before speaking.

'If'n you mean do I own this place, why don't you

say so?' replied the man. 'That's mighty high-falutin' talkin' fer anyone, let alone a negro.' Caleb simply smiled and extended his hand which was pointedly refused.

'Caleb Black,' said Caleb by way of introduction. 'The Reverend Caleb Black.'

'Reveren'! A negro preacher,' muttered the other man looking Caleb up and down. 'Didn't think preachers wore guns or carried rifles,' he continued. 'Yeah, I heard there was such things as black preachers, never thought I'd ever get to see one though. Negroes is rarer'n buzzards' teeth in these parts an' black preachers is even rarer.' He studied Caleb for a few moments more. 'I seen a couple of negroes once, a few years ago back in Hazel. You sure don't look no different from them 'ceptin' you is dressed better'n they were.'

'Are black preachers supposed to look different?' asked Caleb, ignoring the reference to his guns.

'Don't rightly know that,' replied the man. 'I ain't never met any preacher before. I seen one or two from a distance but I ain't never actually met one before, an' I'm reckoned to be more'n seventy years old. My ma was never into all that religion an' stuff an' I guess I just took after her.'

'Reckoned to be over seventy?' asked Caleb.

'Well now, I ain't never had no schoolin' or book learnin' but my ma did teach me to count. She's been dead about twenty years an' she said I was fifty somethin' just before she died, so I reckon that makes me more'n seventy.'

'I can't argue with that,' agreed Caleb, grinning. 'Well, now your education has been completed by meeting a preacher and a black preacher at that, for the first time.' The man did not see any humour in the comment. Caleb decided that neither man was capable of seeing humour in anything as they stared blankly at him. 'As a matter of fact,' he continued, 'I am looking for a young woman. It is my belief that she passed through here recently. I don't suppose you have seen her?' Experience had taught him that people like these two men rarely admitted to seeing or hearing anything.

'Yup!' said the owner of the store, much to Caleb's surprise. 'She was the first stranger through here for more'n six months, now you is the second. All in the space of two days as well. Gettin' to be just like the old days, folk, in an' out of town all the time. We had lots of women in town in them days too. Yes, sir, we had us some real good lookin' women in Emerson before the gold ran out.'

'Two days?' prompted Caleb.

'Yup!' replied the store owner. 'She came through yesterday afternoon. Leastwise I think it was yesterday. It could've been the day before I suppose. Time don't mean that much these days.'

'It must have been yesterday,' said Caleb. 'Did she have anything to say?'

'Nope, leastwise not to us except she bought some coffee an' jerky,' said the second man. 'Jed's wife insisted on servin' her. She never did trust Jed anywhere near another woman on account of he can't keep his hands to himself. Only person she talked to proper was Red Fox. He was the Indian you saw. She talked to Red Fox for some time. Yeah, now I come to think of it she looked just like a squaw but then again she looked like a regular white woman. Anyhow, it looked like she an' Red Fox could talk the same language. Only words of English he knows are whiskey, beer, yes an' no. They was havin' a good talk though.'

'I'm not surprised,' said Caleb. 'Where can I find this Red Fox? He seems to have disappeared.'

'Could be anywhere,' shrugged the store owner. 'Sometimes we don't see him for a week or more an' sometimes he hangs about for a week or more. I hear he's got a cabin up in the hills. Don't know where though an' nobody ain't never bothered to find out. He's an outcast from his tribe I think. When he comes to town he usually trades a few furs for a couple of bottles of whiskey an' drinks himself unconscious. I reckon your woman must've paid him to do somethin' 'cos he bought a couple of bottles for cash yesterday an' there ain't no other way he could've gotten hold of real cash money.'

Caleb had the feeling that Esther was covering her back and that she had paid Red Fox to watch out for either him or, more likely since she probably believed him to be dead, Ephram Barnes. It was more than probable that Red Fox was now on his way to some prearranged meeting place.

'How far is it to the next town?' he asked.

'Quincy,' replied the owner. 'Just keep on ridin' for another two days an' you can'y miss it.'

'Quincy?' said Caleb. 'What kind of a place is it?'

'Bigger'n Emerson, that's fer sure,' laughed the second man. 'Leastwise bigger'n Emerson is now but not as big as it used to be before the gold ran out. They even got themselves a real hotel in Quincy. Emerson had one of them once.' He pointed to a tumbledown building across the street. 'That was it right there. It closed down when the gold ran out, just like most other things closed down. Now there's only about ten of us left in town an' about another twenty or so up in the hills.'

'Not much good for business,' said Caleb.

'I gets by,' muttered the owner. 'Most strangers buy a couple of drinks when they pass through,' he added pointedly.

'Unfortunately I am not a drinking man,' said Caleb, not wishing to even taste the home-made concoctions he believed would pass for beer or whiskey. 'Neither have I any need for supplies.'

'It ain't often strangers ever want anythin' more'n a drink,' said the owner. 'That woman you is after, she's a mighty fine lookin' woman. She mean somethin' to you'?'

'She has something I want,' replied Caleb. Both men leered. 'I do not mean her body,' continued Caleb. 'I thank you, gentlemen. Since there does not appear to be anything to detain me, I shall continue my journey.'

'Just one thing,' said the second man. 'I reckon Red Fox has gone off to tell this woman that you've turned up. Take a word of warnin', Reveren', you just he ready for Red Fox. It could be that she's also told him to kill you, or if not she most likely will when he tells her.'

'He can't be too far ahead,' said Caleb.

'He ain't got no horse but he'll be in Quincy long before you, that's for certain,' said the store owner. 'He'll cut across the mountains an' like most Indians he can keep up a steady jog for most of the day an' hardly be winded. You just take care, that's all.'

'I thank you for your concern,' said Caleb.

'We ain't concerned what happens to you,' the

second man assured him. 'It's just that we don't want no lawman snoopin' around here. Folk in Quincy seem to think we is nothin' but trouble for some reason.'

'Then I shall take great care not to involve you,' said Caleb. 'Good day to you, gentlemen.' He mounted his horse and continued his journey westward.

Quincy was indeed larger than Emerson – which was not too difficult – but even so it was not a large town. It did boast a hotel going by the original name of The Quincy Hotel and it was here that Esther had finally decided to make a stand. She was the only guest. She had come to realize that if she were ever to enjoy the money in her possession, she would have to eliminate Ephram Barnes. Since time was on her side she was quite prepared to wait and see if Ephram did manage to pick up her trail. To that end she had cultivated an acquaintance with two of Quincy's less reputable characters.

For fifty dollars each, they had agreed to kill anyone she wanted killed and in the absence of Quincy's sheriff, who was apparently on business in Sacramento, a city about a week away, they had assured her that the job was as good as done. She had been expecting Ephram and when Red Fox turned up with the news that Caleb was still on her trail, she had serious second thoughts about making a stand. However, she decided that it was also as good a time as any to ensure that Caleb was also dealt with – permanently. She gave twenty dollars to Red Fox and instructed him to go back along the trail and eliminate Caleb. She also promised him another twenty dollars if he succeeded. She then found her two hired guns, Will Downs and Horst Gruber and explained the change of plan and target just in case Red Fox failed.

'Preacherman, you say,' said Horst Gruber. 'That is not good, it is bad luck to kill a priest.'

'A *negro* preacher,' she emphasized.

'It don't matter what he is,' said Will Downs in support of his companion. 'Killin' a preacher is still bad luck.'

'You promised to kill anyone I asked you to,' she said. 'I gave you fifty dollars each. If you are not prepared to honour your part of the deal, I want my money back.'

'Then you'll have to ask Frank, the bartender, for it,' laughed Will. 'OK, I guess me an' Horst have had our share of bad luck so a bit more won't make no difference. We'll kill this preacher of yours for another fifty dollars apiece.'

'I've already paid you fifty dollars,' objected Esther. 'It's hardly my fault if you've both spent it on drink.'

'Lady,' sneered Gruber, 'that's your tough shit. One thing you have to learn out here is that when you pay a man to do a job, you do not give him all the money at once. We have just upped our price by fifty dollars each. You can take it or leave it, we do not care which. One dead preacher will cost you another fifty dollars each.'

'Very well,' she said. 'I shall pay you what you ask – after you have killed him.'

'I reckon you told that Indian to kill him as well,' objected Will Downs. 'You pay us first, that way we get our money no matter who kills him.'

'You kill him, you get the money,' insisted Esther. 'If someone else kills him, you don't. That's all I have to say on the matter.'

After leaving Emerson, Caleb followed the trail for the remainder of that day. He camped for the night alongside a fast-flowing stream and continued the next day. Despite being in the mountains, there did not seem to be much chance of getting lost. The trail wound along several valleys and only once did he see anywhere where he might have taken a different route. During that time he saw no other signs of life other than birds and the occasional squirrel. However, towards evening, he had the distinct feeling that he was being followed.

There was nothing he could point to as proof, it was simply a feeling and he had learned that while he did not get such sensations very often, when he did it was very unwise to ignore them. Bearing this in mind, that evening he made camp alongside a small lake with a large expanse of open space, in the hope of making it more difficult for anyone to surprise him. In his mind there was little doubt as to who was following him – the Indian, Red Fox.

Much to his surprise, there was no attempt on his life during the night. However, if it had been his intention to deprive him of sleep, Red Fox had certainly succeeded. Caleb was quite convinced that he had not closed his eyes at all. Almost as soon as the first weak rays of dawn filtered down into the valley, Calleb resumed his journey.

A short time later he was quite convinced that he had seen the flash of a faded, blue cavalry jacket slip among the trees ahead of him. He drew his rifle and laid it across his legs in front of him and gently eased both his Colt pistols in their holsters. When he reached the spot where he had seen Red Fox, he stopped, looked into the forest, saw nothing and then called out.

'I know you are there, Red Fox. Don't go trying anything stupid.'

'Red Fox not stupid,' came the unexpected response.

'Back in Emerson they said you couldn't speak English,' said Caleb.

'They know nothing,' replied Red Fox, obviously close by. 'I serve many years as scout and messenger for army. I speak English pretty damned good.'

'So I hear,' said Caleb. 'OK, you have the advantage on me. She Who Makes Trouble must have told you to kill me. What's keeping you?'

'You know her Indian name,' replied Red Fox, apparently surprised. 'She told me to kill you, she pay me. She tell me to kill preacher. I no like killing preacher, it bring bad luck. I also know you. I see your face somewhere before, long time ago. I never forget face but I not remember where.'

'You were in the army?' asked Caleb. 'I was too. I was a lieutenant in charge of a black unit. I spent some time in California.'

'Now I remember,' grunted Red Fox. 'Lieutenant Black. Black man named Black I bring messages from headquarters. I see you but never speak to you, only to your sergeant. You not a preacher then.'

'I am now though,' said Caleb. 'You still have the advantage, Red Fox. I'm sure you know how to use a gun. Why don't you use it? That's what you were paid to do, wasn't it?'

'Go in peace, Lieutenant,' came the reply. 'You find She Who Makes Trouble pretty damned fast. She make plenty trouble for herself in Quincy.'

'Meaning what, exactly?'

'Meaning too many people know she carries much money,' said Red Fox. 'They will kill her and take the money. You look for two men, Will Downs and Horst Gruber. I think they work for She Who Makes Trouble but I think not for long. I think they will kill her and take money,. Maybe even now they take her and the money. Such men like to take woman first.'

'I wouldn't he surprised,' said Caleb. 'Just one more thing. I think she thought I was dead. Did she tell you to look for someone else?'

'Ephram Barnes,' replied Red Fox. 'She tell me he a very bad man who wants to kill her.'

'She's not lying about that,' said Caleb. 'If he catches up with her she'll die for certain. She took that money from under his nose.'

'It was his money?'

'No, it was stolen from a bank,' said Caleb.

'I think maybe something like that,' said Red Fox.

'I don't know how much she paid you,' said Caleb. 'But if you knew how much she had, you might even have tried killing her yourself.'

'I think many thousands of dollars,' said Red Fox. 'Pretty soon Downs and Gruber find out. They will kill her as easy as they tread on cockroach if they find out. Why do you follow her?'

'As well as being a preacher, I am also a bounty hunter,' said Caleb. 'I want the reward for taking that money back.'

'It is strange, a holy man who kills for reward,' said Red Fox. 'I know two other men who hunt for reward, but they are not preachers.'

'Even holy men must make a living,' said Caleb.

'This man, Ephram Barnes,' said Red Fox. 'You want me to kill him?'

'No, not particularly,' replied Caleb. 'I think I can deal with him myself.'

'Then go find She Who Makes Trouble before Downs and Gruber kill her and take the money,' said Red Fox. He stepped on to the trail in front of Caleb. 'Remember, beware of Downs and Gruber.' He suddenly turned and disappeared amongst the trees again.

Caleb had intended to ask how far it was to Quincy but had missed the moment. However, judging by the fact that Red Fox had been to Quincy and back, on foot, it seemed that it was not too far ahead.

By nightfall, Caleb had made camp at the head of a valley overlooking a large lake perhaps four or five hundred feet below and about five or six miles away. It was after total darkness had closed in that Caleb realized that he was also overlooking what could only have been the town of Quincy. At what must have been the edge of the lake, he saw the glow of many lamps. He was tempted to complete the journey there and then, but decided to leave it until the following morning when he could make the steep descent in daylight.

Down in Quincy, Will Downs and Horst Gruber huddled over glasses of beer, talking about Esther and her apparent wealth.

'I say we take her,' said Downs. 'I reckon that carpet-bag she came to town with is full of money. I reckon there could even be more'n a thousand dollars.'

'What about Sheriff Crocker?' asked Gruber. 'He is just looking for any excuse to either kill us, have us hanged or at least sent to prison.'

'He ain't here, remember,' hissed Downs. 'That deputy of his ain't no bother. Ain't you noticed, he never goes out at night. I think he's shit scared of the dark.'

'I don't like it,' said Gruber. 'So far we've managed to keep out of trouble and I am getting used to the idea of not having to keep running.'

'Well we'll sure have to run pretty fast if we kill this preacher feller,' reminded Downs.

'You know we never intended to kill him,' said Gruber.

'Yeah, I know that,' said Downs. 'The thing is, that woman's really loaded. Just think of it, with that amount of money we wouldn't have to stay here. We could even go to Mexico or maybe Canada. Hell, I'll bet my life that that money is stolen. Why else would she pay folk like us an' that Indian to kill folk followin' her.'

'I don't want to kill her,' insisted Gruber.

'We don't have to,' said Downs, laughing. 'If that money is stolen, who the hell is she goin' to complain to when we take it? She can't, not without gettin' herself arrested.'

'It might not be stolen,' said Gruber.

'For that kind of money, I'm prepared to risk it,' said Downs. 'You an' me could get a long way on a thousand dollars. Trust me, Horst, I know there's at least a thousand, there has to be, believe me.'

EIGHT

An hour after sunrise, Caleb slowly rode down the main street of Quincy. His arrival seemed to cause something of a sensation, particularly amongst the many small children. It seemed obvious to him that all of them, as well as many adults, had never seen a negro before. Some of the smaller children ran to the protection of their mothers' skirts whilst a few of the older, braver ones, followed him along the street, some even asking him if his skin really was black. He simply smiled and ignored their remarks, although he did find it unusual. The adults, for the most part, simply stood and stared, remaining silent. A few of the smaller children were obviously frightened, all the more so when heard a couple of mothers tell their children that if they did not behave, the black man would take them away and eat them. He was tempted to admonish these mothers but then thought better of it. It would only serve to make life more difficult.

He pulled up outside the hotel, dismounted and then, quite deliberately, smiled at the people now crowding round. His smile had the effect of making some at the front retreat to the rear and at least two

112

men place themselves between the stranger and their wives. He laughed and made a point of removing his rifle and carrying it into the hotel as a precaution against theft since he had no doubt that rifles were just as expensive here as anywhere else and always liable to disappear if left unattended.

The small, timid-looking man behind the desk was plainly confused and seemed almost frightened as Caleb approached. Some of the crowd had plucked up enough courage to mount the board-walk and peer over the top of, or even under, the swing doors as if expecting something to happen.

'I assume you folk round here have never seen a black man before,' Caleb said to the man.

'No . . . no, sir,' responded the man. 'I mean . . . well some folk have but I've lived here more'n twenty years an' you're the first I've ever seen in this territory.' He licked his lips nervously. 'What can I do for you, sir? If it's a room you're lookin' for I guess we can find one.'

'I might take you up on that,' said Caleb. 'Actually I'm looking for someone. Since I understand this to be the only hotel in town, I have to assume that the person I am looking for is here or has been here.'

'Yes, sir,' replied the man. 'Who might you be looking for?'

'A woman,' said Caleb. 'A woman called Esther.' He thought for a moment. It had only just occurred to him that he did not know Esther's other name. 'I have to admit that I do not know her full name, I simply know her as Esther. I suppose she could be calling herself Esther Barnes.'

'Esther Barnes,' said the man, opening a book, donning a pair of spectacles and pretending to look very important. 'Would that be Mrs or Miss?'

'I don't see that it matters much,' said Caleb. 'Is that the register?' He did not wait for a reply but took the register and looked through it. 'I wouldn't have thought you would need to check, it looks as though you only have one guest, a Mrs E Smith. Hardly an original name, is it?'

'Yes, sir . . . I mean no, sir,' responded the man, recovering his precious register 'Smith is a pretty common name in these parts. There's at least twenty of them in town.'

'Perhaps so,' said Caleb. 'Which room is she in?'

The man seemed to pluck up some courage, almost defiantly raised himself to his full height – which was considerably less than Caleb's – and squared his shoulders. 'That's confidential information, sir,' he said. 'We respect the privacy of all our guests. May I ask who wants to see her?'

'You may,' said Caleb with a broad grin. 'You can tell her the Reverend Caleb Black wishes to speak to her.'

'Reverend!' gulped the man. A rather large woman suddenly appeared from a room behind the desk. 'You hear that, Charlotte, this er . . . man claims to be a minister. He wants to see Mrs Smith.'

The woman was plainly not intimidated by Caleb's colour or calling. 'I heard,' she snarled. 'The question is does Mrs Smith want to see you? What possible business could a white woman have with a negro, even if he is a minister?'

'My business is strictly private,' replied Caleb. 'As to whether or not she wants to see me, I suspect that answer would be in the negative. Not wanting to see me and actually refusing are different things. Why don't you ask her?'

'I suppose that means she wouldn't want to see you,' grunted Charlotte. 'At least you talk like a minister, usin' words most folk can't understand. You just hang on here, I'll go tell her you've arrived, if she don't know already. It seems everyone in the county knows, goin' by the crowd outside. I can't allow you up into her room, it wouldn't be proper for a negro to be alone with her.'

'But it would be proper for a white man?' said Caleb.

'I seen negroes before,' replied Charlotte. 'In Sacramento. I seen the way they looked at white women. You just hang on here. Silas, if he so much as makes one move, you shoot him.' She suddenly bent down and took a pistol from under the counter which she handed to her husband. Silas meekly obeyed and, very shakily, pointed the gun at Caleb. Caleb simply laughed and casually pushed the barrel to one side.

'You just be careful, Silas,' he said. 'Those things have a nasty habit of going off when you least expect them to and they might even hurt someone.'

'Yes, sir,' said Silas. 'I know that, sir. You just do like my wife says an' you won't get hurt.'

'I wasn't thinking of me,' said Caleb, nodding at the faces behind the door. 'I was thinking of one of them.' He deliberately exposed the gun on his right thigh. Silas gulped and backed away a few paces, the gun in his hand now shaking so violently even Caleb was worried. Charlotte simply snarled something and thundered up the stairs.

A couple of minutes later Charlotte thumped

back along the corridor, calling at the top of her voice. 'Silas, you go call Sam Doherty, tell him to get his lazy ass over here at the double!' She leaned over the rail at the top of the stairs and glared down at Caleb. The rail creaked ominously and visibly moved under her weight. 'I don't know who the hell you are, mister,' she called. 'But I reckon you got some questions to answer.' Before she could say anything else, Caleb ran up the stairs. In the confusion Silas appeared at a complete loss.

'Where is she?' demanded Caleb. He did not wait for a reply but ran along the corridor to a room to which the door was open. He was closely followed by the now breathless Charlotte.

The body of a woman lay on the floor, her skirts in disarray and torn. Although it was obvious that it was Esther, her face was badly bruised and bleeding. Caleb bent down and placed his ear close to her mouth.

'She's still alive!' he pronounced. 'She needs a doctor.'

'I'll say if she needs a doctor or not,' a voice at the door said. Caleb turned to see a middle-aged man pointing a gun at him. 'You all right, Charlotte?' he asked. 'I'd heard about a negro comin' into town an' I was just on my way over.' Charlotte nodded. 'Stand up,' ordered Deputy Sheriff Sam Doherty. 'Real slow an' drop your guns.'

'Sheriff,' sighed Caleb, standing up but ignoring the order to discard his weapons. 'This woman's hurt, can't you see that? She needs a doctor.'

The deputy glanced at Esther and nodded to Charlotte. 'Go get Doc Bruce,' he said. 'I'll keep this feller covered until you get back. Maybe then someone'll tell me just what the hell's goin' on round here.' Charlotte clattered from the room and Doherty stared at Caleb. 'I said, drop them guns. Don't you understand English?'

'Sheriff,' sighed Caleb, 'perhaps I should introduce myself. I am the Reverend Caleb Black, a minister of the. . . .'

'Go shit!' snarled Doherty. 'Since when did preachers carry fancy firin' pieces like that? I said, drop them guns.' He threateningly raised his pistol slightly.

Caleb once again sighed and obediently placed his rifle on the floor, followed by the exposed gun on his right thigh. Sam Doherty relaxed somewhat, relaxed enough for Caleb to take his chance. An instant later the deputy was looking down the barrel of Caleb's other Colt.

'Now, Sheriff,' Caleb said, very quietly. 'I think we ought to get a few things straight. First of all, lower that gun unless you intend using it. However, I can assure you that you will be dead before you can even squeeze that trigger.' Doherty gulped and obediently lowered the gun, eventually replacing it in the holster. 'Now, as you know, I have only just arrived in town so I would have thought that even you would realize that I could not possibly have had anything to do with what has happened here. It is obvious that she was beaten quite some time ago, the blood on her face has dried. It is true that I came here looking for her, I admit that. It is also true, despite your incredulity, that I am indeed a minister of the church and that my name is the Reverend Caleb Black. I will also admit that as well as being a minister, I supplement my living by bounty hunting. It is in this capacity that I have followed this woman all the way from Broken Ridge, not far from Kernville.'

'Bounty hunter!' gulped Doherty. 'I guess that explains the guns. First time I ever seen a man wearin' two guns. I heard of folk like you, but this is the first time I ever seen any man with two pistols. You sure had me fooled. Is she wanted by the law?'

'No, strictly speaking she is not,' said Caleb. 'It would take too long to explain. You will just have to take my word for it that she is involved, indirectly, in a bank robbery which took place in Kernville.'

Further questions by Sam Doherty were interrupted by the arrival of Doc Bruce, closely followed by Charlotte. Charlotte saw Caleb's gun and looked at the deputy questioningly; who shrugged and grinned weakly. Charlotte glanced upwards and sighed in obvious disgust. Caleb replaced both his Colts and picked up his rifle.

'She'll live,' pronounced Doc Bruce. 'She's taken a severe beating, that's all. I don't think there are any bones broken. Get her on to the bed, I shall have to examine her further just to be sure.' Caleb and Sam Doherty lifted Esther on to the bed. The doctor started to unbutton her clothing but, after a sharp cough from Charlotte, he turned to look at Caleb and the deputy. 'I think, gentlemen, that it would be inappropriate for you to remain. I shall call you, Sam, when I have completed my examination.' Sam and Caleb obediently left the room. Charlotte remained to supervise Doc Bruce.

The lobby was now full of people, all of whom asked questions when they saw Sam Doherty. Sam raised his hands to silence them.

'Nothin' to concern you folks,' he said. 'The lady

who was stayin' here has had an accident, that's all. Now, please clear out, there's nothin' for you here.'

'What about him?' demanded a voice. 'Seems kinda strange to me that she has an accident as soon as he appears in town.'

'This is the Reverend Caleb Black,' said Doherty. 'It is true that he came looking for the woman but the accident had nothin' to do with him, he's only just arrived, remember.'

'Reveren'? said the voice. 'I ain't never heard of a negro preacher before.'

'Well you have now,' said Caleb. 'The Good Lord, in His infinite wisdom, recognizes black people as well as white as His children.'

'Blacks is only fit for slaves,' said another voice. 'I know, I lived down South once. That was all blacks was fit for.'

'There was a recent war, remember,' said Caleb. 'Slavery is a thing of the past, we are all equal in the eyes of the law and the eye of God.'

'Still don't seem right to me,' replied the voice. 'What kind of accident did she have, Sam?'

'Somebody tried to beat the hell out of her,' replied Doherty. 'Leastways that's what it looks like. Doc Bruce is with her now. Now, please go home or about your business.' The crowd slowly dispersed, almost every one of them looking suspiciously at Caleb.

'Sorry about the reception, Reveren',' apologized Doherty. He held out his hand which Caleb accepted. 'Sam Doherty, Deputy Sheriff. The sheriff is on business down in Sacramento. He ain't due back for another week.'

'I am sure you are doing an admirable job, Mr

Doherty,' said Caleb. 'Now, have you any idea why anyone should have attacked Esther – Mrs Smith as she apparently calls herself – and, more importantly, who?'

Whilst he had been in the room, Caleb had glanced around looking for the carpet-bag but had not seen it. It was always possible that it was in a cupboard somewhere, but he had noticed that a wardrobe had been ransacked. The wardrobe was the most likely place for her to have stored the bag. He chose not to tell the deputy just how much money Esther had been carrying. However, it seemed obvious to him that someone had discovered her secret and it was also plain to him just who that someone was.

'I wouldn't know,' said Sam. 'She came into town a couple of days ago I suppose. I never actually met her myself. As far as I know she was no trouble. I reckon Charlotte Stebbings is the best person to ask.' He laughed drily. 'There ain't nothin' goes on in the whole of Quincy County that she don't get to hear about even before it's happened sometimes.'

'It would appear that a negro is something of a rarity,' said Caleb, looking at two small boys peering under the swing door. 'I am surprised.' He pulled a face at the children who screamed and ran off.

'I've lived here all my life, some forty-five years, an' I ain't never seen one in these parts before,' admitted Doherty. 'I seen a couple in Hazel a few years ago when I was that way. I hear tell there's plenty in Los Angeles an' San Francisco, but I ain't never been to either place. Now if you'd been an Indian nobody would've given you a second look. A negro though, that's a different matter. We just don't get your kind up here.'

'Are you sure you haven't heard of anyone she was friendly with?' said Caleb, probing just in case there was someone else involved. 'My information is that she got talking to two men, Will Downs and Horst Gruber.'

'Then you know a darned sight more'n I do,' grunted Doherty. 'For a man who's just arrived in town you sure seem to know a hell of a lot.'

'I have my informants,' said Caleb. 'Have you seen either of these men recently?'

'They was in the bar last night,' said Doherty. 'I can swear they was there at ten o'clock last night, I saw 'em myself.' He thought for a moment. 'Come to think of it though, they was actin' kinda strange. Mind, at the time I didn't think much of it, they always acted strange after a couple of drinks. Maybe Silas can tell you somethin', he was servin' behind the bar last night.' As if to order, Silas suddenly appeared behind the desk. 'Silas,' said Doherty. 'Will Downs an' Horst Gruber. I thought they was actin' strange last night. Did you notice anythin'?'

'Could be,' replied Silas, looking questioningly at Caleb.

'Well were they or were they not?' asked Caleb. 'It could be important.'

'Yes, sir,' gulped Silas on receiving a nod from Doherty. 'The fact is they've been acting very strange this past couple of days. Normally it's as much as they can afford to buy a glass of beer between the both of them a couple of times a week. Yes, that's right, I hadn't thought about it before. Mrs Smith arrived and that very same night they both had more money than they knew what to do with. I ain't complainin' mind, that's what I'm in business for, but they were suddenly spending money, lots of money. I reckon they must have spent about a hundred dollars in two days. That's more'n they ever spent in a whole year before.'

'Money which she paid them to take care of either me or a man named Ephram Barnes,' said Caleb. 'Probably she told them to look out for Ephram Barnes, she already thought she'd killed me.' He indicated the wound on his forehead.

'You think she hired them to kill you?' said Doherty. 'I can't believe they'd do somethin' like that. Sure they're a couple of bad 'uns. They'd beat a man or steal anythin' but I can't see either of them murderin' anyone.'

'Then I suggest that you find out if they are still in town,' said Caleb. 'I suspect though that you will discover they left town either last night or early this morning.' Doherty looked questioningly. 'Esther – Mrs Smith – had a large amount of money when she arrived. When the doctor has finished his examination, I shall return to her room and look for it. I doubt very much if I shall find it.' He addressed Silas. 'I don't suppose that she gave you a carpet-bag or any other bag to look after?'

'No, sir,' replied Silas.

'That's about their mark,' said Doherty. 'A lone woman with plenty of money. OK, I'll go see if they're still in town.'

Doc Bruce and Charlotte came down the stairs just as Sam Doberty left the hotel. Charlotte stared coldly at Caleb as the doc told him that apart from a severe beating and signs that she had been raped, there were no other obvious injuries. He told

Charlotte that he would be along later in the day to see the patient again but that in the meantime she was to be kept very quiet. Caleb did not ask permission, he simply bounded up the stairs, followed by a protesting Charlotte. Caleb ignored her protests and burst into the room.

He also ignored Charlotte's protests as he searched the room for any sign of the carpet-bag or any other bag. As expected, he found nothing. Esther was plainly still unconscious but the blood had been cleaned from her face. Charlotte attempted to bar Caleb's way as he left the room, demanding an explanation for his behaviour, but was pushed, quite gently, to one side.

Sam Doherty was back in less than twenty minutes with the news that the shack in which Downs and Gruber had lived was now empty and that their horses had also disappeared.

'George Welbeck – he owns the general store – reckons he saw two men who could well have been Downs and Gruber ridin' out of town just before dawn,' said Doherty. 'George opens his store at five-thirty on the dot every mornin' 'cept Sunday when he don't open till eight,' he explained. 'He thought it was unusual for anyone to be leavin' town that early, but he didn't bother too much about it.'

'Which way?' asked Caleb.

'West,' said Doherty. 'There's only two ways you can go from here. Back east the way you came or west followin' the lakeside for about four miles. There's another road about ten miles out which heads down to Sacramento, they could've taken that. Personally, I don't reckon they would though. That way they might run into the sheriff an' if they have taken this money, he's the last person they'd want to meet. They know he'd know somethin' was wrong. I reckon they'll take the road over the Pandosa Pass an' out towards Redding. Once they get to Redding there's three or four ways they could go.'

'And they were seen at about five-thirty this morning,' said Caleb, glancing at the large clock in the lobby. 'It's now nine-fifteen, almost four hours' start. I don't suppose they will ride too fast, I could catch up with them by mid-afternoon.'

'I'd go with you,' said Doherty, 'but I was told not to leave Quincy on any account.' Caleb was actually pleased that the deputy would not be with him and from the deputy's manner he too was plainly not very sorry. 'You should catch up with 'em OK. The horses they got are a couple of broken down hacks, it'd kill 'em if they was to break out into a gallop.'

'It would be better if you remained here anyway,' said Caleb. 'I'm not the only one looking for Esther. You just keep an eye on things here. I'll be fine. In particular you keep an eye open for a half-breed negro called Ephram Barnes. Whatever you do, don't let him anywhere near Mrs Smith.'

'You got it,' agreed Doherty. 'I know I said I didn't think they'd ever kill anyone,' he added, 'but if they have found themselves as much money as you say. . . .'

'I never said how much,' corrected Caleb.

'No, I guess you didn't,' conceded the deputy. 'Anyhow, I reckon it has to be a goodly amount else you wouldn't be tryin' to get it back. The thing is, although they ain't killers, I guess enough money can turn even the most timid man into a killer. You just watch what you're doin'.'

'I can look after myself,' assured Caleb. 'Just one thing. Have you any idea how good they are with guns?'

'I suppose they learned a thing or two when they was in the army,' said Doherty. 'Will Downs used to say that he an' Gruber met when they were servin' with the cavalry. I did hear though that they weren't in the cavalry at all. They was in the engineer corps accordin' to a stranger who came through couple of years ago. He'd served with them. I never seen either of 'em use a pistol or a rifle, so I don't really know.'

'Doc Bruce thinks that they might have raped her,' said Caleb. 'I'll make sure they both come back to answer the charge and stand trial. I assume rape is illegal in these parts? Mind you, I suppose they can only be charged if she makes a formal complaint. Somehow I have my doubts if she'll be prepared to do something like that.' At that moment Charlotte leaned over the rail at the top of the stairs and called down.

'She's come to. I told her you was here lookin' for her. She said for me to send you up.'

'Thank you,' said Caleb. 'I'll be right up.' He looked at the deputy. 'Just remember, don't allow Ephram Barnes anywhere near her.'

It was very difficult to tell if Esher was pleased to see Caleb or not. The bruising round her mouth made it difficult for her to be understood. Charlotte waited at the foot of the bed and Caleb did not try to get her to leave the room. He placed his ear close to Esther's mouth and listened intently.

'Took the money...' she whispered. 'Trusted them ... been such a bloody fool ... took all the money....'

'I know,' replied Caleb. 'I also know where they are. I'll get it back. You take it easy. You've been hurt pretty bad.'

She apparently attempted a smile and slowly raised a hand to touch the wound on his forehead. 'Tried to kill you,' she croaked. 'Glad I didn't. You are a good man . . . make some woman very happy.'

'I do not think I am quite ready for that yet,' said Caleb. 'The closest I want to get to being married is to conduct a wedding ceremony for someone else. You have been very foolish, She Who Makes Trouble. This is the second time you've almost been killed. You might not survive a third time.'

'We'll see,' she said defiantly, attempting a weak smile. 'There's still Ephram to deal with.'

'Then I hope I'm back before he arrives,' said Caleb.

NINE

Dozens of pairs of curious eyes followed Caleb as he rode out of town and immediately he had disappeared from view most citizens were crowding round the sheriff's office demanding to know what was going on. To his credit, Sam Doherty refused to answer.

Sam had been correct about there being only one way out of Quincy, apart frorn the direction Caleb had entered. A narrow strip of land followed the lakeside and any thought of leaving the track would have been impossible since the mountains rose almost sheer. After about four miles the track turned inland, through a narrow valley. From there the trail rose quite steeply but it was plainly well used and fairly easy going.

Looking for signs that Downs and Gruber had travelled that way was something quite beyond Caleb's tracking abilities and he did not even try. He did not actually force his horse into a gallop, although he did not travel too slowly. Less than an hour after he had left Quincy he reached the point

where the trail divided. Fortunately for him there
was a sign indicating that the left-hand fork led to
Sacramento and the right to Redding. In neither
case was there any indication as to how far it was to
the places named. As suggested by Sam Doherty,
Caleb took the right fork to Redding.

About three hours later, Caleb came across an
isolated farmhouse set a few yards back from the
trail. An elderly man and two youths, each armed
with ancient muzzle-loading rifles, had obviously
witnessed his approach and were standing outside
the stone cabin.

Although armed, their attitude appeared more
one of curiosity than confrontation and, contrary to
the reaction of the people of Quincy, they did not
seem surprised at his colour. It might have been that
Caleb misread the situation, but there was something about the whole thing which told him that
something was not quite right and he was prepared
for trouble. He quite deliberately exposed the gun
on his right thigh and cautiously moved forward. He
noticed that one of the youths shuffled uneasily,
licked his lips and furtively glanced at the older man
as if awaiting instructions. The old man remained
completely impassive other than to spit on the
ground.

'Good morning,' greeted Caleb. 'I wonder if you
have seen two men pass this way this morning? You
might even know who they are. Will Downs and
Horst Gruber from Quincy.'

'Who wants to know?' demanded the older man.

'The Reverend Caleb Black,' said Caleb with a
broad smile. An elderly woman appeared at the
door, looking suspiciously at the stranger. Caleb

touched the brim of his hat and nodded at her. 'Good morning, ma'am,' he said. 'I was just asking if two men had passed this way recently?'

'I heard,' she muttered. 'Reverend, you say? What in the name of hell is a reverend doin' out this way, especially a black reverend?'

'He's askin' about Downs an' Gruber,' explained one of the young men.

'I ain't deaf,' grumbled the woman. 'I got ears. What you want 'em for?'

'A little unfinished business,' said Caleb.

'Can't see what kind of business men like them could have with any preacher,' she said. She studied Caleb closely for a moment. 'You sure you is a preacher?' Caleb nodded. 'First time I ever seen any preacher wearin' a gun.'

'Even a minister of the church needs to protect himself sometimes,' said Caleb. 'Have you seen these two men?'

'We seen 'em,' grunted the elderly man. 'Maybe three hours ago. They didn't stop though.'

'Hush your mouth!' commanded the woman, obviously annoyed that the man had confirmed that Downs and Gruber had been there. 'OK, they was this way,' she confirmed with a resigned sigh. 'Must be the first time in years they left Quincy. They in some kind of trouble? Mind, I guess that wouldn't be too difficult, they'd steal anythin' what wasn't tied down.'

'They could be,' said Caleb. 'It all depends on whether or not you consider raping a woman being in trouble.'

'Rape!' the woman laughed scornfully. 'I don't reckon either of 'em would know what to do with a woman if she laid herself out in front of 'em. Who in the name of hell are they supposed to have raped?'

'Well I can assure you they have just discovered how,' said Caleb. 'The woman is a stranger in Quincy, although she is known to me. I have been following her for some time. I thank you for confirming that I am on the right trail. I had thought perhaps that they might have turned off towards Sacramento.'

'If they is guilty of rape,' snarled the woman, 'you go find 'em, Reveren'. Last rapist we had in these parts was hanged. I would've thought that was more in the sheriff's line of business though, not a preacher's.'

'The sheriff is apparently on business up in Sacramento,' said Caleb. 'Deputy Sam Doherty claims that he has been given instructions not to leave Quincy for any reason at all. That's partly why I am following them.'

'Sam Doherty don't need instructions not to do anythin',' scorned the woman. 'It's all he can do to get his ass out of bed. You must be the first negro most folk in Quincy've ever seen.'

'I believe that is so,' nodded Caleb. 'We are apparently a rare breed in these parts.'

'One is one too many,' muttered one of the youths.

'Hush your mouth!' snarled the woman. 'You just show a little more respect for a preacher no matter what colour he is. You go find 'em, Reveren',' she said.

'They ain't ridin' fast.' She laughed sardonically. 'On them horses they couldn't ride nowhere fast. You'll probably catch 'em up in the Pandosa.'

'The Pandosa Pass?'

'Ain't nowhere else,' muttered the elderly man. 'Unless you is a mountain goat, only way through is through the Pandosa.'

'How will I recognize it?' asked Caleb.

'Don't you worry none about that, Reveren',' said the woman. 'You'll know when you've reached the Pandosa. Mind, once you're there, findin' 'em could be a different matter. A whole army could hide out up there an' never be found.'

Since it appeared that there was little else to be gained by asking them any further questions, Caleb touched the brim of his hat and urged his horse forward. For some considerable time, he was conscious of being watched and was aware of one of the youths climbing the side of a hill and on to a large outcrop to watch. He rode on, pretending that he had not seen the youth.

Caleb was far from happy; there was something about the situation at the farm which did not ring true. There was nothing he could put a finger on, more a feeling. A feeling which would not go away. The woman had more or less said that the chances of his finding Downs and Gruber up in the Pandosa were very remote. He had the distinct feeling that his chances were less than just remote. He was suddenly convinced that they were nil. He was unable to explain even to himself how he knew, he just did. He knew that the men he was following had never reached the Pandosa Pass. Exactly where they were, or if anything had happened to them, he obviously did not know, but he did know that to continue would be a waste of time. He suspected that it was also what the woman wanted him to do.

He rode very slowly for another fifteen minutes just to make certain that he was no longer being watched before stopping to double-check.

Although it was quite possible that someone could have been hiding among the myriad of rocks and trees, he had the feeling that he had not been followed very far. It seemed that the folk from the farm were convinced that he was heading for the Pandosa. Deciding to take a chance, he turned and slowly rode back towards the farm. When he considered himself to be fairly close, he dismounted and led his horse among a group of trees and rocks and tethered her to a bush. Taking his rifle, he then cautiously made his way back along the trail, eventually reaching the outcrop where he had last seen the youth. Taking great care not to make a noise, he scaled the outcrop and lay on the top looking down on the farmhouse.

At first there was nobody to be seen; however, the view showed the rear of the farmhouse quite clearly. There were a few outbuildings with hens scratching about, two pigs rooting around in a small field part way up the side of a hill, a few sheep scattered about the open hillside and, most significantly, a small paddock containing at least six horses and a cow. It was the number of horses which surprised him, not the cow.

He knew enough about horseflesh to know that at least two of the horses were draught horses. Two others appeared to he young draught horses, although he might have been wrong. The remaining pair were most definitely riding animals even if they were not in very good condition. He sensed that these animals did not belong to the owners of the farm but were the horses ridden by Downs and Gruber.

Caleb weighed up his options. At that moment he had absolutely no proof that the two men he sought were at the farm, but he was quite convinced that they had not proceeded beyond it. Since time seemed to be on his side, he settled down to wait. He did not have to wait too long.

Ten minutes later the two youths appeared, went into the paddock and led one of the large draught horses to the side and eventually reappeared with the animal now in harness and hitched to a buckboard. The woman came out and spoke to the youths and then all three went into the house. The youths emerged again a couple of minutes later prodding their guns into two men who, although he had never met them, Caleb knew to be Will Downs and Horst Gruber. The men were forced to sit on the buckboard under the watchful eyes of the youths.

His initial instinct was to run down to the farm but he knew that even armed as they were with ancient muzzle-loading rifles, he would not be able to storm the building with any degree of certainty. He continued to watch for some time. The old man came out and, pointing along the trail towards Pandosa Pass, was apparently giving final instructions. The two horses which he had assumed belonged to Downs and Gruber were also brought round and hitched to the buckboard. Caleb suddenly decided it was now time to retrieve his own horse.

Having untethered his horse, he led her further up the hill where he waited, overlooking the trail.

Eventually the buckboard came into view, the two youths riding up front, one of them turning occasionally to threaten the two men. From what Caleb could see it certainly appeared that both men had been quite severely beaten. He waited another ten minutes after the wagon had passed before making his move.

'There ain't that much money in the whole world!' exclaimed the old man. 'I know you had some schoolin' an' learned to count but you gotta have it wrong.'

'Then you count it if you is so damned clever!' snarled the woman as she lovingly fingered piles of notes. 'I tell you there's more'n thirty-seven thousand here.' She picked up a bundle and flicked through it, her eyes gleaming. 'Hell, with this kind of money we can get the hell out of here. We could go to 'Frisco or maybe even Los Angeles. I always fancied Los Angeles myself.'

'It's stolen money,' said the man. 'It has to be. I'll bet my life that was what that negro preacher was after.'

'It don't matter if'n it's stolen or not,' said the woman. 'Right now it's right here, on this table an' it belongs to us.'

'It probably belongs to that woman they was supposed to have raped.'

'An' where did she get it from?' she sneered. 'OK so it's stolen money. My bet is she stole it from someone else. Either way, as I see it, neither her nor Downs an' Gruber is goin' to shout too loud. That preacher happened along at the perfect time. If anyone comes lookin' they'll probably know Downs an' Gruber stole it from the woman. We tell 'em that they passed through here followed by the preacher. If they do find Downs an' Gruber they sure ain't goin' to admit that they stole it an' the law will think that the preacher took the money off them. All we have to do is sit tight for a while.'

'I say we get the hell out of it as soon as we can,' said the man.

'We sit tight for a while,' she insisted. 'We carry on like nothin' has happened. After a couple of months maybe then we can leave, but not before.'

'I don't like it,' muttered the man.

'Then you got two choices,' she sneered. 'Run like hell now, on your own, or stay here. I don't much care which. If you leave, you leave without any of the money.' She looked up at the man and laughed. 'Go on, get the hell out of it. With this kind of money I can probably buy me a young, virile man. It'd sure make a change.'

'Supposin' that preacher comes back?' said the man. 'Supposin' he finds Downs an' Gruber an' they tell him what happened? Supposin' he comes back here an' kills us all?'

'Supposin', supposin'!' sighed the woman. 'You've spent all your life supposin' this, that an' the other. OK, so there is a chance he'll be back, that's something, we'll have to deal with if an' when it happens. We all got guns. That's four against one. I don't give much for his chances. Maybe you ain't never killed a man before but I have. Two to be exact. Believe me, it was easy. If you don't have the guts, I have. They'll never be able to find his body, not up here.'

'I still don't like it,' grumbled the man.

'It wasn't the kind of scenario I had in mind

either!' Both of them spun round and found themselves looking down the barrel of Caleb's Colt. 'You were right, old man,' he continued, easing the door closed behind him. 'It is stolen money. It was stolen from a bank in Kernville.'

'An' you've been chasin' it ever since,' sneered the woman. 'I guess even a reverend can forget his principles when there's this much money involved.'

'My principles are still intact,' said Caleb, picking the carpet-bag off the floor and placing it on the table. 'Every penny of this will be returned to the bank in Kernville. I shall be satisfied with the reward. Now, put it all back into the bag.'

'And if we don't?' challenged the woman.

'As you say,' said Caleb with a broad grin, 'Nobody would ever find your bodies up here.'

'Preachers don't kill folk, they save their souls,' she said.

'Sometimes it is necessary for someone to die in order that their soul might be saved,' said Caleb.

'You wouldn't!' croaked the man.

'Are you prepared to try me?' answered Caleb. 'I can assure you that I have killed men before and as your woman rightly says, it is very easy.'

'You ain't no preacher!' snarled the woman. 'You is a bounty hunter. All bounty hunters is the scum of the earth.'

'That might be so,' admitted Caleb. 'I am indeed a bounty hunter, but I am also an ordained minister of religion. A man has to make a living somehow. Now, unless you want me to prove I can and will use this gun, put that money in that bag.'

'Go shit!' she snarled.

Caleb's Colt spat forth its message and the woman clamped her hand to her ear but did not scream. Instead she glared hatred at Caleb.

'Next time it will be straight between the eyes,' said Caleb, coldly.

The man immediately set to, grabbing at the money and stuffing it into the carpet-bag. The woman simply sat glaring at Caleb as she applied a dirty cloth to her bleeding ear. Eventually all the money was in the bag. Caleb laughed and picked it up.

'Just one thing,' he said. 'Not that it bothers me what happens to them, but where are your boys taking Downs and Gruber? I gather that you beat them up before taking the money.'

'Not far,' scowled the woman. 'Just far enough to make sure they keep on ridin' an' never come back.'

'Someone once said to me that this amount of money could even turn a saint,' said Caleb. 'They might very well come back. I almost wish I could be here to witness their return. I shall now return to Quincy. I shall tell Sam Doherty what good and honest citizens you have been in rescuing the money from those men. I shall also tell him that it was your intention to hand the money back to him, that you were only looking after it until it could be returned to its rightful owner.'

'Go shit, Reverend,' she snarled. 'You'd better have eyes up your ass all the time you is in Quincy County.'

Caleb laughed and opened the door. 'Haven't you heard? All negroes are born with eyes up their arses!' He spoke to the man. 'Now, just in case you have any ideas about shooting me, you take those two rifles outside and lay them where I can see them. Are there any more guns in the house?' The man glanced at the woman and shook his head. 'Which neans that there are,' continued Caleb. 'Well just don't get any idea about using them. I can assure you that I am an excellent shot with either hand.' He flicked aside his coat to reveal the gun on his left thigh. The man gulped, picked up the rifles and followed Caleb outside where he placed them on the ground. Caleb glanced at a window and fired, the bullet shattering the wood-work. 'I warned you, no guns!' he said. There was a tirade of cursing and swearing from inside the cabin.

Caleb quickly mounted his horse and galloped off. He was aware of a shot being fired but knew that by that time he was well out of range of the muzzle-loaders. He kept up a sustained gallop for about ten minutes before allowing his horse to revert to its more accustomed leisurely walk. He felt reasonably certain that he would not be followed.

Caleb's return to Quincy caused as much interest and comment as there had been when he had arrived the first time. Sam Doherty actually managed to pull himself out of his rocking-chair outside the sheriff's office and amble along to the hotel. It seemed to be a well-known fact that the carpet-bag Caleb carried contained a lot of money and the main topic of conversation and speculation was now on exactly how much. Guesses varied wildly, some even talking in millions, although most had no idea what a million really meant.

'I reckon I oughta take charge of that,' said Sam Doherty when he met Caleb in the lobby of the hotel. 'I reckon it's what they call evidence.'

'Evidence of what?' asked Caleb.

'Well,' said Sam, plainly on uncertain ground. 'There's been a crime committed here an' the sheriff is allus tellin' me to make sure I collect the evidence.'

'What crime?' asked Caleb.

'Why, rape of course,' said Sam. 'Doc Bruce is quite certain she was raped.'

'Has she made a complaint?' Caleb asked.

'Er . . . no, no sir, I guess she ain't. Leastways not yet she ain't. Doc Bruce has been to see her an' he says she ain't to be questioned just yet.'

'Then we'll wait and see if she does make a complaint,' said Caleb. 'In the meantime this bag stays with me.' He banged heavily on the bell on the counter. 'Anybody there?' he called.

'We heard you,' grumbled Charlotte, coming from the back room. 'What you want now? If it's her you want to see, she ain't fit to see nobody. Doc Bruce gave her somethin' to make her sleep.'

'A room,' said Caleb. 'Since it appears that I shall have to stay here tonight, I might as well do so in comfort.'

'Two dollars!' grunted Charlotte. 'Find your own meals.'

'Expensive!' said Caleb, nodding knowingly. 'Most places charge one dollar a night.'

'Two dollars!' Charlotte repeated impassively. 'Take it or leave it. Two dollars in advance.'

'Two dollars!' sighed Caleb, digging into his pocket and producing the required amount.

'So what happened to Downs an' Gruber?' asked Sam Doherty.

'They are still alive, if that's what you mean,' said Caleb. 'At least they were the last time I saw them. They are probably up on Pandosa Pass by now. I don't suppose they will bother coming back to Quincy.'

'They sure won't be missed,' said Doherty. 'Did you meet up with the Blincoe family?'

'The farm on the way out to the Pandosa?' said Caleb. 'Yes, I met them. I must admit I have had better welcomes.'

The deputy smiled and shook his head. 'All I can say is you is damned lucky to be alive. If they'd known you had that money I wouldn't've put it past Ma Blincoe to have you killed.'

'Actually,' said Caleb. 'They were most helpful.' Sam Doherty stared at him in disbelief.

Caleb was shown a room which, he was not surprised to discover, was about as far away from the room occupied by Esther as it was possible to be. He waited about half an hour before venturing along two corridors to Esther's room. He was surprised to find her awake and sitting up in bed.

'I thought I heard your voice,' she said as he entered the room. 'You were a lot quicker than I expected.'

'And you are much better than I expected,' said Caleb. 'I have the money. I shall be returning to Kernville in the morning. What are you going to do?'

She looked at him rather surprised. 'Aren't you taking me back as well?'

'I had considered it,' he said. 'You are, of course,

at liberty to come with me if that is what you want. I do not think it is really necessary though. As far as I am aware there is no warrant out for your arrest. Even if there is, I do not think it will achieve much.'

'I don't want to go back to either Kernville or Broken Ridge ever again,' she said. 'If you're not going to force me to go back, I think I'll carry on to San Francisco. It's one place I've always dreamed about goin' to.'

'You won't have any money,' Caleb pointed out. 'How will you manage?'

Esther laughed. 'I'm a very experienced woman,' she said. 'I know what men like. Don't you worry none about me, Reverend. My name is She Who Makes Trouble, remember? I was brought up as an Indian an' like most Indian women, I know how to survive.'

'I have no doubts that you will,' agreed Caleb, grinning broadly. 'A word of advice though. When you leave here, take the Sacramento road. I have the feeling that it will he a lot safer.'

'You are speaking from experience?' she asked. Caleb nodded. 'OK,' she agreed. 'I had more or less decided on goin' that way anyhow. I can maybe make a few dollars in Sacramento.'

Caleb looked at her almost fondly for a moment before taking a wallet from his jacket pocket. He pulled out nine fifty-dollar notes and fifty dollars in fives and tens which he handed to her.

'I think I owe you that much at least,' he said. 'It ought to last you until you reach San Francisco and then some. Perhaps you can set yourself up in some kind of business.'

She squeezed his hand. 'That'd be nice,' she said.

'Somehow though, I reckon there's only one business I'll ever be any good at.'

'Then set your standards high,' advised Caleb.

'Only the best!' She laughed.

TEN

The following morning, Caleb was on his way even before George Welbeck had opened his store. He had deliberately planned it so, partly to avoid Deputy Sam Doherty, but mainly to avoid seeing Esther again. He was not very good with emotional farewells and he sensed that Esther could be very emotional.

Apart from its raining for most of the way, his journey back as far as Emerson was completely uneventful. When he did arrive in Emerson it was almost as if time had stood still in the small community. It appeared that the same woman was washing the same clothes and that the two men had not moved a muscle, sitting in front of the store in exactly the same positions as they had occupied on his previous visit. Since it was still only midday, Caleb did not bother to stop. He simply rode by, acknowledging the two men as he did so. For their part they just gazed at him, the only indication that they had seen him being the store owner lifting his hat and scratching his head and apparently saying something to his companion.

The rain ceased at about mid-afternoon, although
Caleb did find the going rather more difficult than
before due to swollen rivers, a very muddy track and
numerous cascades of water from the surrounding
hills and gully-sides, some of which he was obliged to
actually pass under.

Despite the conditions, he appeared to make
good time and reached the cabin where he had left
the bodies of the two men at about the time he had
expected. The two horses were still hobbled and
grazing and the bodies of the men had apparently
lain undisturbed by either man or beast, although
there was a very definite aroma of death about them.

He spent that night in the cabin and, leading the
horses with the bodies across them, started out for
Hazel shortly before dawn the following morning.

The one thing which had surprised him was not
having met Ephram Barnes. He had been quite
certain that Ephram would have discovered which
way either he or Esther had gone and set off in
pursuit. It was beginning to look as though he had
been wrong.

Once again, his destination of Hazel was reached
without trouble and even crossing the Smoke Creek
Desert proved easier than on the outward journey. It
had apparently also rained in the desert and even in
such a short time long hidden plants had blos-
somed. There was also no shortage of water. The
first thing he did on arrival in Hazel was take the
bodies along to the sheriff and explain who he was
and what had happened.

'Small beer!' sighed the sheriff. 'Hardly worth the
bother of bringin' 'em in. Sure, there is a reward out
on 'em, fifty dollars apiece. Still, I guess a hundred

dollars ain't so bad, 'specially since you say you had to kill 'em anyhow. Come back in an hour, I should have the money by then.'

'No problem,' agreed Caleb. 'There is something else I wanted to ask. When I was in town last, there was another man who was also following the same woman I was. His name is Ephram Barnes. Have you any idea what happened to him? I'm certain he didn't take off towards Emerson or Quincy.'

'The half-breed negro,' said the sheriff with a knowing smile. 'Sure, he's still here.'

'Still here?' queried Caleb.

'Yup,' grinned the sheriff. 'Right here. Him an' a few others are out repairin' the road south at the moment. It got washed away in the rain a couple of days ago. We got a local ordinance here in Hazel which states that if a man don't pay his gamblin' debts, he ends up in jail. He gets one week hard labour for each fifty dollars or part of fifty dollars he owes. Your man owed one hundred so that means he got two weeks.' He glanced at a book on the desk. 'That means his time's up the day after tomorrow. Do you want to see him?'

'Not particularly,' said Caleb. 'The other thing is, do you know when the next train east is?'

'Tarriopah,' said the sheriff. 'As far as I know that's due out day after tomorrow. I can't be sure what time though an' with the weather as it has been down track it might even be the day after that 'fore it gets through. They'll tell you more down at the railroad station.'

Caleb thanked the sheriff and went along to the railroad station where he discovered that the next train to Tarriopah was indeed in two days' time.

They did not appear to have any information as to whether or not the train would be on time or indeed if it would actually arrive. However, he booked himself and his horse on the train.

His next call was at the Sylvester household, where Mrs Sylvester fussed around him like a large mother-hen, insisting that after his long journey he must have a hot bath and some food. The bath he was very pleased to accept, the food he was a little more dubious about, hoping that she would not go to the extent of cooking him one of her specialities. She was, in fact, most apologetic; all she had was some steak-pie and greens. Caleb was more than relieved.

'I'll try an' cook somethin' decent for tomorrow,' she promised. 'I knows how you liked my plantains an' puntkin.' Like many people, she seemed to have difficulty in pronouncing the word 'pumpkin' and it invariably came out as 'puntkin'. 'Trouble is they both have to come through by railroad an' it seems like the weather's been too bad where they is grown.'

For once Caleb actually gave thanks for the rain. 'Steak-pie will do just fine,' he assured her.

After his most welcome bath and steak-pie, Caleb decided to go back to the sheriff's office and collect his hundred dollars. It was as he was leaving the office that he encountered a gang of men being led back to the jail. Among them was Ephram Barnes.

'You!' snarled Barnes. 'You is just about the last person I expected to see. I'd've thought you would've taken the money an' got the hell oul of it. I assume you caught up with Esther.'

'I did and the money is quite safe.' Caleb nodded.

'I had expected you along but I see you were unavoidably delayed.'

'Damned stupid law!' snarled Ephram. 'Still, I'm out of this in two days.' He suddenly laughed. 'Hell, maybe I did myself a favour. I didn't have to go lookin' for the money, it's come home to me.'

'It doesn't belong to you,' reminded Caleb. 'I intend to see that it gets back to the bank in Kernville.'

'Mad!' sneered Ephram. 'Like most preachers, you is completely mad. You've got your hands on more money than you'll ever see again in your life an' it's yours for the takin'. Hell, if I was in your shoes I'd be a long way from here by now, somewhere they don't know me an' don't know or give a damn about where the money came from.'

'But you are not in my shoes,' commented Caleb. 'I wouldn't go back to Broken Ridge or Kernville if I were you. I don't think you'll be very welcome.'

'Tell me something I don't know!' sneered Barnes. Further conversation was cut short by a deputy ordering Ephram into the jail.

Two days later, Caleb went along to the railroad station only to discover that the train to Tarriopah had been delayed for twenty-four hours due to repairs to the line. Although he was annoyed at the delay, Caleb realized that there was nothing he could do about it and returned to the Sylvesters. Later that day, Ephram Barnes was released.

'Naomi ain't come home yet,' said Mrs Sylvester. 'It ain't like her.'

'Perhaps she is working late,' said Caleb.

'I sent the boy to find out,' she said. 'He just got

back an' she ain't there. He was told she left at her usual time. Something's wrong, I knows it is, I can feel it. She ain't never been late before.'

'Perhaps she is visiting friends.'

'I thought of that,' she said. 'The boy's gone to see. I don't think so though, she's a good girl, she don't do things like that without tellin' me.'

'I'm sure everything will turn out all right,' assured Caleb. 'It is a long time since I was her age, but I do know I didn't always tell my parents everything.'

'No,' said Mrs Sylvester. 'I knows she has her secrets, like all girls her age. This time though I knows somethin' is wrong.'

'Well until you know for certain that she isn't with friends there is nothing you can do,' said Caleb. 'We'll talk about it when your boy returns.' Half an hour later the boy did return with the news that Naomi had not been seen since leaving work at the hotel.

'Mr Black, sir,' the boy said to Caleb. 'While I was out lookin' for Naomi this feller asked me if you was stayin' here. I said you was, I hope I did right.'

'Sure thing, son,' said Caleb. 'Who was this man?'

'He didn't say his name, sir,' said the boy. 'He said you'd know who he was.'

'Was he a black man?'

'I guess so,' nodded the boy. 'Leastways he looked black, but then again he looked like a white.'

'Ephram Barnes!' sighed Caleb. 'Yes, I'd forgotten he was being released today. What else did he say?'

'Nothin' except to tell you to meet him in the Diamond Saloon in half an hour.'

'Thanks, son,' said Caleb.

Half an hour later Caleb approached Ephram Barnes in the Diamond Saloon. Ephram pushed an empty glass at Caleb.

'Mine's a whiskey,' he said.

'Then I suggest you buy it,' said Caleb. 'You wanted to see me.'

Ephram grinned and nodded for Caleb to follow him to a table. 'With all the money you got I would've thought you wouldn't mind buyin' a feller a drink.' Caleb remained silent. 'That money is what I've come to talk about,' Ephram eventually continued. 'That an' a certain young black lady who's gone missin'.'

Caleb moved in his chair and leaned forward. 'Right now there's a gun aimed straight at your balls,' he hissed. 'What do you know about Naomi Sylvester?'

'Come now, *Reverend*,' said Ephram, grinning broadly. 'That wouldn't be very Christian, would it? Besides, I haven't got a gun so how would you explain shooting my balls off?'

'I said, what do you know about Naomi Sylvester?' Caleb hissed again.

'Pretty girl, very pretty,' said Ephram. 'I could sure do things with her. The thing is, Reverend, I'm quite sure you wouldn't want anything to happen to her. Right now she's perfectly safe. I'll come straight to the point. You get her back, unharmed an' still a virgin – if she is a virgin – in return for that money.'

'I'll see you in hell first,' Caleb grated.

'Maybe that's just where we will meet again,' said Ephram, 'even though you is a preacher. The girl for the money, them's my terms.'

'All I have to do is call the sheriff,' said Caleb. 'In fact I believe he's already been informed that she is missing.'

'Do that,' invited Ephram. 'You don't think I'd be here talkin' to you if I wasn't sure the girl would be dealt with do you? I'd thought of that. Right now she's bein' looked after by three sex-starved fellers, one black, two white. Don't you worry none about her fer now though, she's safe enough. The thing is, if I don't get back to 'em in another half-hour, they've been told they can do just what the hell they like to her. That means they'll kill her to stop her from identifyin' anyone. After they've had their fill of her of course.'

'A four-way split of the money,' said Caleb. 'Personally I would have expected you to want the lot.'

'Well, they think it's goin' to he a four-way split,' agreed Ephram with a broad grin.

'I see,' said Caleb. 'You get the money, I get Naomi and your friends get a bullet in the back.'

'I don't think you need worry about the details,' said Ephram. 'Oh, don't bother having the town searched, she isn't here. I'm not that stupid.'

'You appear to have thought of everything,' said Caleb. 'If I should agree, where do I take the money?'

'You don't,' said Ephram. 'We meet again, in this saloon, in two hours. You bring the money with you.'

'And Naomi?'

'She'll be safe,' said Ephram. 'I tell you where to find her.'

'And your friends?'

'I'll deal with them,' muttered Ephram. 'Now,

Reverend, do we have an understanding?'

'An understanding, yes. I'm not sure if I agree or not.'

'I don't give a damn if you agree or not,' hissed Ephram. 'You got two hours. Just remember, no money, no girl. I'll leave you to explain to her parents how it happened. Personally, unless I've greatly misjudged you, I don't see you just allowin' a perfectly innocent girl to be raped an' murdered. I'm not bluffin', Reverend. My three friends are only too anxious to get their hands on her and they will kill her. I know they will, they've done it before.'

'If they haven't raped her already.'

Ephram shrugged. 'That's a chance you'll just have to take. At least she'll be alive. Two hours, no more. Now I must go and tell my friends that everything is working out as I planned. Oh, an' just in case you thought about involvin' the sheriff, don't. If I so much as suspect a trap, the girl dies.' Without another word, Ephram left the saloon. Caleb was not very far behind, just in time to see Ephram riding out towards the south.

On his way back to the Sylvesters he met the sheriff and established that Ephram had been released along with two white men and one negro and that none of them had been seen in town since their release.

An hour later, Caleb was still trying to work out how to ensure that Naomi was returned safely *and* that the money remained in his possession. He had been tempted to inform the sheriff but he had not told him about the money and he did not want it known. He had just about resigned himself to having to hand over the money when the Sylvester boy knocked timidly on his bedroom door.

'Mr Black, sir,' gulped the boy. 'I don't know if this'll mean much to you, sir, but you know that man what said he wanted to see you?' Caleb nodded. 'Well, sir, an hour or more ago, I was in the street opposite the saloon when I seen him come out.' Caleb remained silent. 'Well, sir, I don't know why, but I took it on myself to follow him.'

'He was riding a horse,' said Caleb.

'Yes, sir, I knows that,' replied the boy. 'I is a pretty fast runner, I can beat most anyone in town when it comes to runnin'. Well, sir, I follows his horse. I knows where he's livin'.'

'Where?' demanded Caleb.

'In a shack down by the railroad marshallin' yards,' said the boy. 'I seen him go inside. I waited maybe ten minutes but he didn't come out again.'

'Did you see anyone else in the shack?' urged Caleb, placing his hands on the boy's shoulders and staring him in the face. 'Think, son, it is important.'

The boy was plainly frightened. 'I didn't mean no harm, sir,' he choked. 'I thought I was doin' the right thing.'

Caleb suddenly smiled and gently squeezed his shoulders. 'Sure, boy, sure, and you did do the right thing. But think, was there anyone else in the shack?'

'I . . . I . . . I don't know, sir, I didn't get that close.' He faltered.

'No, you did the right thing,' said Caleb. 'Were there any other horses outside the shack?' Whilst he was asking questions Caleb was fastening his two gunbelts and checking that both pistols were loaded.

'I don't think so, sir,' said the boy. 'I don't know for sure though.'

'Right, come with me,' said Caleb. 'You show me exactly where this shack is. He almost dragged the boy out of the house, calling to his mother that everything was going to be all right.

On the way, with the boy by now very frightened, Caleb called at the sheriff's office but found it locked. There was an elderly man sitting outside the store next door to the office and Caleb told him to tell the sheriff that he was down at the marshalling yards and to get himself down there as fast as possible.

A short time later Caleb was hiding behind a freight wagon studying the shack identified by the boy. The boy himself had been despatched to make certain that the sheriff was aware of what was happening.

There were four horses close by the shack and, since it was now dark, a faint light could be seen through the grimy window. He had also expected the sheriff by this time but it was plain that the message had not reached him. He glanced at his watch. It was now almost time for the meeting of himself and Ephram in the saloon.

A door suddenly opened and a familiar shape emerged to mount a horse and head towards the town. In the absence of the sheriff, Caleb decided that it was now time to make his move. Quite how he was going to tackle the three men apparently still inside the cabin, he was not at all certain. As far as he was concerned the most important thing was the safety of the girl. He slowly wandered across various rail lines until he was outside the shack, both his

Colts at the ready.

At first he peered through the small window and saw Naomi bound to a chair. There appeared to be three other men, as Ephram had claimed, although Caleb did notice that only one of them wore a gunbelt. That was not to say that the other two did not each have a gun since it was quite common for guns to be simply stuffed into the tops of trousers.

Seeing the horses suddenly gave Caleb an idea; he quite deliberately spooked one of them in an effort to make it seem that Ephram had returned. It appeared to work as one of the men called out, 'That you, Ephram?'

'Sure,' replied Caleb, doing his best to imitate Ephram's voice. 'Worked like a dream, the money's all here.' The door suddenly opened to a loud 'Whoop' and two of the men dashed out.

Caleb's Colts spat forth their lethal message; both men fell to the ground, one clutching briefly at his chest and staring, wide-eyed, at Caleb. The other, although again wide-eyed, obviously did not see a thing and did not feel much, if anything. The hole in his temple slowly oozed blood as his head hit the ground.

'I'll kill her!' screamed a voice from inside the shack. 'Back off or I'll kill her, whoever you are.'

'You kill her and you are a dead man for certain,' warned Caleb. 'Give yourself up now and perhaps you will only have to answer a charge of kidnapping. At least you are still alive which is more than can be said for your friends here.'

'Ephram!' said the voice, now almost hysterical. 'What happened to Ephram, what's he done with the money?'

'He hasn't got the money,' said Caleb. 'You never expected him to share it with you, did you? If I had handed it over he would have probably killed all three of you or at least got out of town as fast as possible leaving you to deal with the girl and the law.'

'Bastard!' came the rather more composed reply. 'I warned 'em, they can't say as I didn't warn 'em. I never trusted that man. OK, mister, I'm comin' out. I'll leave my gun on the chair, so don't shoot.'

Caleb took a step backwards as the door opened a little wider and the negro appeared. At first the man appeared very surprised to see Caleb. He had obviously been unaware of Caleb's colour.

'The Reverend Caleb Black,' muttered Caleb. 'Preacher and bounty hunter.'

'Yeah, I remember now,' growled the man. 'I seen you when you was in town before. OK, so you is a bounty hunter. I got news for you, there ain't no bounty on my head or theirs, so you might as well let me go.'

'That's up to the sheriff,' said Caleb. He turned his head slightly to listen. 'Sounds like he's here now.'

Caleb was wrong; a bullet suddenly tore through the crown of his hat, grazing the top of his head and sending him crashing to the ground. Suddenly Ephram was above him, astride his horse and his gun aimed at the now defenceless Caleb.

'Now you all die!' hissed Ephram. 'First you, Reverend, then him, then the girl. I'm really goin' to enjoy killin' you. . . .'

Caleb automatically braced himself as a shot rang out but the expected impact never occurred. Instead

Ephram was suddenly falling off his horse on top of him. A short time later the body was pulled off and Caleb looked up into the face of the sheriff.

'Sorry I couldn't get here sooner,' the sheriff apologized.

As on the outward journey, suspicious faces peered at Caleb as he reclined in the comfort of the first class carriage and once again he simply smiled at them. At Tarriopah he changed trains and was surprised to discover that he had the first class compartment all to himself for the entire journey. He wondered if word had got around or if it was simply that first class passengers did not often travel to Kernville.

Naomi Sylvester had been uninjured in any way. It transpired that she had left the hotel by the back door, as she usually did, but had suddenly been attacked by at least two men, gagged and bundled into a large sack before being thrown across a horse. She had had no idea where she had been taken.

The sheriff had been out of town but had been accosted by the boy immediately on his return. It had been pure chance that he had reached the shack in time.

Nobody was more surprised than Deputy Marshal Barnaby Wells when Caleb presented himself at his office complete with all but $624 of the stolen money.

'I've got to admit, I misjudged you,' he said. 'I'm not surprised you found Esther and the money but I had you down as takin' it for yourself.'

'Let's just say that it was a great temptation,' admitted Caleb. 'I'll settle for the reward though.

That way I won't have to keep looking behind my back.'

Shortly after he had convinced the president of the bank that the missing money had not been taken by him, he collected the reward and wandered along the street. On turning a corner, he suddenly came face to face with another preacher – a black preacher, although a man much younger than himself. Both men stared at each other for a while and eventually the young man spoke.

'You must be the Reverend Caleb Black,' he said, offering his hand. 'I was told that there was another black minister in the area. Samuel Makepeace, I've come to take over the ministry at Broken Ridge.'

Caleb suddenly laughed out loud. 'I heard,' he said. 'Mrs Maud Higgins told me you were coming. Fine woman, Mrs Higgins. She must be about eighty years old but don't you go calling her just Mrs Higgins. She likes folks to use her given name of Maud. You just remember that, son, *Maud* Higgins.'

'Yes, sir,' said the young preacher. 'Thank you for the information.'